"Just as chicklit heroine Bridget Jones struggles with men, retired anti-hero Bernard Jones is bemused by the trials and tribulations of investing. Anyone who is a member of an investment club will instantly recognise the characters in this clever, well crafted and highly amusing book."

Brian Durrant, Investment Director, The Fleet Street Letter.

"In Bernard Jones, Nick Louth has produced an anti-hero for our financial age. Whether it is fighting his way to a secure retirement, jousting with the council over wheelie bins or feuding with his wife over his fondness for cakes and biscuits, Bernard Jones goes into battle on behalf of us all."

Matthew Vincent, Editor, Investors Chronicle.

"Bernard Jones, tried by life, marriage, family, friends and neighbours as much as by investment is a must-read. He's on the way to becoming a minor classic."

Chris Crowcroft, Investors Chronicle reader

"I have enjoyed reading Bernard Jones Diary as he attempts to enjoy retirement with a mixture of cunning and (not too much) knowledge. I wish him well."

Eric Cox, Investors Chronicle reader

D1329345

"It's so easy to identify with Bernard Jones and the situations he describes. I almost feel I know him as a friend. His diary is the first page I turn to in the magazine. It is always topical and hugely entertaining."

Leonard Spark, Investors Chronicle reader

"Bernard and I are soul mates…We share the same hopeless investing traits being driven by misty-eyed emotion, alcohol and a love of chocolate rather than the cold logical appraisal of information so beloved by the professionals.

Gordon Gray, New Zealand

"I have found myself laughing out loud and occasionally in giggles!"

Mark Hobhouse, Investors Chronicle reader

A must read for the private investor…Share the highs and lows of life with Bernard as he battles the twin imposters of triumph and despair (not in equal measure unfortunately).

Tony Watson, Investors Chronicle reader

Nick Louth is a financial journalist, author and investment commentator. He has regular columns in the Financial Times, the Investors Chronicle and on MSN Money website. His previous book, investment guide *Multiply your Money* was published by McGraw Hill in November 2001. Nick Louth is married and lives in rural Lincolnshire.

Funny Money

The Investment Diary of Bernard Jones

By Nick Louth

"The funniest and most realistic book ever written about investment" – Investors Chronicle

Ludensian Books

www.nicklouth.co.uk
www.bernardjones.co.uk

The Bernard Jones Diaries

Published by Ludensian Books
242, Eastgate LN11 8DA

ISBN 978-0-9554939-0-4
Printed by TradePrint Europe 2007

ISBN 978-0-9554939-0-4

9 780955 493904 >

For Louise

Design and cover by DAB Graphics
Illustrations by Samara Bryan

Foreword

Welcome to the first collection of Bernard Jones investment diaries. Bernard Jones originally began as a one-off feature idea for the Investors Chronicle for the Christmas edition of 2005. The plan, to leaven the magazine's share tips and analysis with some light-hearted comic fiction, worked so well that editor Matthew Vincent asked me (actually I didn't need much persuading) to revive Bernard as a weekly and topical column for the magazine.

This book is more than a collection of previously published columns. A good quarter of the book is new and unpublished material. It also includes many of Samara Bryan's wonderful illustrations, which so brought to life the domestic crises which propels Bernard from one furiously scribbled diary page to another. Never in the field of human conflict have so many biscuits mattered so much to so few, as Churchill may once have said.

The next volume of the diaries, *Bernard Jones and the Temple of Mammon* will be published in November 2007, and a sample chapter is to be found at the back of this book.

Those who want to follow Bernard's adventures week-by-week will find a subscriber offer to the Investors Chronicle in this book. There is more background information on Bernard Jones and the other characters at the website www.bernardjones.co.uk and on the Investors Chronicle's own site www.investorschronicle.co.uk.

Nick Louth

December 2006

Introduction

Retired civil servant Bernard Jones isn't, as he would be the first to agree, the world's greatest investor. Like many people who decide to delve into the world of shares in search of a financially secure retirement, he finds everything more baffling, less profitable and a great deal more time consuming than he imagined. Why is it that a company can produce sparkling financial results, but the share price immediately drops on the news? How is it that profit warnings come along, like London buses, in threes? How is it that his friend and former colleague 'perfect' Peter Edgington, who claims to spend only half an hour a week on his low-risk portfolio can consistently out-perform Bernard who spends two hours every day glued to the computer screen. Above all, with all this time and effort why does he lose money so frequently?

Over the months and years, Bernard discovers some of the answers to these questions, but as he taps away on his keyboard in the den at the back of the house more powerful forces are at work. These are not merely the huge but invisible tides of market sentiment sweeping investment values hither and thither, but seismic disturbances closer to home.

Bernard's twenty-something daughter Jemima, a high-flying lawyer living in Fulham with a dull banker named Toby, suddenly flees to return home with her battalion of teddy bears. She bears tearful news that Toby has turned to the arms of another, somewhat hairier, paramour. Bernard's schoolteacher son Brian, principled and pedantic but hitherto steady, takes an uncharacteristic risk for promotion by becoming head of department at a notorious girls' school. Brian's wife, Janet, is troubled by mysterious complaints in what Bernard terms "women's bits".

Bernard's dotty mother, Dot, has been a constant trial for years. Now approaching 90, she still lives in a mental world of ten bob notes and dried egg, where the drone of Heinkel engines is to be expected at any time. Recycling notices to her means only one thing: it's time to stack those old milk saucepans by the parlour door, ready for them to be made into Spitfires. However, when Bernard discovers something of real value amongst Dot's old papers, she suddenly reverts to lucidity to question his motives.

The most dangerous warning signals are always the closest. Eunice, Bernard's wife, is increasingly concerned at her husband's secretive consumption of cakes and biscuits for 'elevenses'. A devotee of ER and Holby City, Eunice believes that dangerous cholesterol, diabetes and congestive heart failure are inevitable unless she acts fast. She decides to tackle the issue head on. Other matters sit ill at ease, too. Eunice ran the household for decades while Bernard was eroded by the daily grind at the Ministry of Defence, but now he is retired his eccentric habits are increasingly disruptive to the world in which she reigns supreme. Though she accepts his tinkerings with the model railway in the loft as merely the quaint diversion for an ageing male, she is much more upset by his continued lack of interest in her even now they have much more time to be together. "I am a woman, Bernard, but sometimes I don't think you even recognise the fact," as she once told him. "And, I have a woman's needs."

For many months, Eunice regarded Bernard as emotionally and sexually dormant, though the arrival of an attractive Danish au-pair next door rapidly changed her appraisal. What transpired then seemed entirely out of character. However, it was Eunice's discovery of Bernard's so-called Investment Diary, in the den's normally-locked Hornby drawer, that really raised the temperature. These jottings, ranging well beyond the world of money and shares, revealed a side of her husband she had never seen. Here, laid out for all to see were his impotent rage at bothersome builders, his frustration at noisy 'low-class' neighbours, his fury at feminist or environmentalist cant, and his complete disdain for anything smacking of political correctness. Much of this she already suspected, but his uncompromising descriptions of her good friends Irmgard and Daphne Hanson-Hart were beyond the pale. Worse still, the fact that he described their young grandson as 'The Antichrist' was truly shocking. Yes, Digby was difficult. Yes, he would eat only three types of food, and nothing without salad cream. That's how children are these days.

But perhaps worst of all was the way he described her.

Here are those diaries.

Acknowledgements

I should like to thank all those who helped me in the research for this book. While the characters and storyline are fictional, much of the investment background against which they develop is factual. I'm particularly indebted to the registrars and company secretary's department at Marconi/Telent for their help in describing the process of tracking an old share certificate.

As always, the responsibility for any remaining errors is my mine alone.

Without the help and assistance of the Investors Chronicle, particularly Matthew Vincent, Rosie Carr and Erica Morgan, this book would not have been possible. David Benson at DAB Graphics was patient with my many demands.

I should like to thank the estate of W. H. Davies for permission to quote from his poem *Leisure*.

Finally, and as always, I should like to thank my wife Louise for her support and encouragement. Let me add, for those who suspect some autobiographical notes in these diaries, that not only I am nothing at all like Bernard, she is nothing like Eunice.

Chapter One

Sticking with it for Good or Ill

Friday 1ˢᵗ April 2005: An unusual attachment

All Fools' Day. In five minutes time it will be exactly 62 years ago to the minute that I, Bernard Jones, forced his way into an ill-prepared world with a yell, a kick and an unexpected shock of hair. Of course that was the last thing to be seen by the midwife, because following a long Jones family tradition I arrived breech first. Though I wouldn't know it for years, this delivery was merely the preparation for a career in the Ministry of Defence where everything is deployed arse-about-face, from the launching of warships, the ordering of radar for Nimrod reconnaissance aircraft, the procurement of the Bowman infantry radio, right through to the self-adhesive floor tiles at the old Admiralty Building. The joke ran that Sir Douglas Gattingford, who was supposedly on temporary attachment, was certain to become the permanent secretary after spending 40 minutes trying to extricate his crepe soles from the stationery office floor.

Still, all that was four years ago. Early retirement, without the long grinding commute to Charing Cross, and the well-rehearsed mutterings and imprecations about punctuality, should have allowed me a little luxury: A lie in, the Today programme on Radio 4 at 8am rather than Farming Today at six, a relaxed cup of tea and a slice of toast heavy with Frank Cooper's thick-cut marmalade. Best of all, a chance to read the Telegraph without having to fold it fifteen times, without having to wedge myself between a witless 7' teenager, wobbling to the tzzz-tzzz-tzzz from his earphones, and some dumpy perfume-drenched VDU operator from Penge decked in more gold chains than Haile Selassie.

I had really looked forward to the days when I no longer had to overhear at 7.45am the mobile phone conversations of 19-year-old shop assistants, pallid breasts bulging out of their mis-buttoned blouses relaying the night's carnal capers: "No, Tania, that was Geoff. Last night was Chris. Eh? No, Chris from accounts. Nah, I wutunt touch 'im from the ware'ouse. 'Ee gave Natalie chlamydia …."

The prospect of early retirement seemed so wonderful, so enticing that the reality hit hard. You see it was only then that I discovered, or rediscovered, that I was married to a woman called Eunice whose demands are every bit as unreasonable, tedious and repetitive as those of the MoD. Now I'm home, it's my job to let Hermès (the cat) in when she cries outside in the morning. What time is that? Quarter-to-bloody-six, that's what time it is. Then the ungrateful animal swaggers past me, casts a dismissive glance at the highly-expensive nutritionally-balanced Moggymix Breakfast Biscuits I have put out for it, and then runs upstairs purring like a dynamo to jump on the bed next to Eunice.

So I often end up listening to Farming Today anyway. Once I'm up, then I might as well make a pot of tea, because Eunice will be awake, grumbling that my "tutting and harrumphing" about the cat had woken her too. As the years go on, I find that I'm sleeping less, so the lie-in has become pointless. Today was a case in point. Brought up a mug of tea to Eunice, couldn't get back into bed without turfing out the cat. Merely suggested that we get a cat flap, so the animal could come and go as it pleases.

"No, Bernard, really. If you build a cat flap you'll get every tom, puss and moggy coming into the house. You know how Hermès gets bullied by that ginger monster from over the back."

Eunice turned to stroke the cat's belly, while it waved a paw coquettishly. "Poor Hermès . You wouldn't even feel safe on Mummy's bed any more, would you, Darling?"

"She's a cat, for Christ's sake! A killing machine refined over ten million years of evolution with teeth and claws for ripping and tearing flesh. There is nothing in the DNA of a sabre-toothed tiger that says some poor bloody caveman had to get up at a quarter to six to give it a saucer of milk and a cuddle."

"Bernard, Hermès is a domesticated animal, not some escapee from Longleat."

"Tell that to the tortured sparrows I've had to pull from its maw. She chews off the flight feathers and the feet and watches the poor things as they flap helplessly. Quite puts me off breakfast."

"Well, we're not having a cat-flap and that's final."

And so it goes. Eunice gets her way, and I relent. After the best part of three decades at home, Eunice is in her element. Everything is arranged just the way she wants, from the anti-macassars on the sofas to the myriad baskets constructed at her evening classes that gather dust on every inch of sideboard, mantel piece and coffee tables, like a legion of refugees from some savannah bondage ritual.

As the Johnny-come-lately I am told I'm in the way in the kitchen, that I clutter up the sitting room and am merely a nuisance in the dining room. I actually can't get into either bathroom except by appointment, and as for the bedroom…well, I tell you about that later. Suffice it to say once Eunice has had a drink or two the threat of hippopotamus manoeuvres is real enough to deter any move into that room. In fact I only feel at home in the den, where I have my desk, PC and investing materials, or up in the loft where my model railway is taking shape.

Monday 4th April: Investing at a run

Investing has for me become something like cross–country running was when I went to St Crispin's: Something I have been told to do for my own good, which I rarely enjoy, and which requires rather more stamina than I had bargained for. And one more thing about investing: Like cross-country I *always* seem to come last. The trouble with owning shares is actually quite simple. It's great fun when prices are going up, and awful when they're going down. Despite what I've been told by those who supposedly know better, there's nothing whatever you can do to influence which of those experiences you get. Look at Railtrack for example. Seemed a fantastic bet when John Major privatised it along with the rest of the railways in 1993. No-one cared about the railway infrastructure it owned, it was the brownfield land that got investors salivating. All that undeveloped waste land around the sidings and marshalling yards, the old disused tunnels, the rights of way, the forgotten weed-strewn acres. Then what happened? October 2001, down comes the whole edifice, pulled into administration when Stephen Byers refused it any more government money. I paid 360p for the shares in 1993, could have sold them for £17 at the peak of the market (why didn't I? I have no idea) and then they were suspended at 276p. I got most of this back eventually, but that was a big comedown from the compensation we should have had.

That was merely a typical experience. My portfolio of shares in 1999 was worth £130,000. Now, six years later it's down to £82,000. Almost every disaster during the great bear market has come to visit me: The split cap debacle, Equitable Life, Railtrack, plus a mis-sold endowment mortgage. Thank God for the MoD index-linked pension. Perhaps the most irritating thing is the

16

hours I have spent, writing down the closing prices, using my old slide rule to calculate returns, jotting down when the dividends are due and all that. I should just have done what my mother does and stick it in Aunty Vi's Burmese teapot.

Wednesday 6th April: Taxing conversations

First day of the new tax year. Plenty of capital losses in the old one to set against future gains, should I ever have any future gains. Eunice has been on at me again about cholesterol, having caught me in the den *inflagrante* with a packet of Scottish shortbread. I had secreted them in the lockable desk drawer where I keep my Hornby catalogues, but once the door opened I was caught like a startled rabbit.

"Bernard, what are you eating?"

"Just a meagre biscuit, Dear, to keep body and soul together."

"There's nothing meagre about that. Do you know how much fat there is in a shortbread biscuit? It's 28 per cent! Come on, you remember what the doctor said. You don't want to end up like my Uncle Giles."

"What, you mean having to move to Slough?"

"No, I mean having a coronary."

"The heart attack that killed him was brought on by a road accident, not by a Walkers shortbread!"

"Well yes, but it was a clot that blocked off his blood vessels."

"The clot in question was the one in the Astra that shot the lights on the Hanger Lane Gyratory System and bent Giles's Peugeot."

"It's not funny, Bernard."

"Oh, I don't know."

"You could easily die, and I'd be a widow!"

Hm. Yes, that would make you think, wouldn't it?

Tuesday 18th April: Gone with the windy

Took my 89-year-old mother to the cinema this afternoon to see a special pensioners' screening of *Gone with the Wind* . This is probably her first cinematic outing since *Ben Hur*. Though the cinema is now an Odeon she keeps referring to it as the Gaumont.

"Ooh, look at the price, Bernard. That's disgusting! Five pounds even with me pensioner discount. In my day it used to be fourpence ha'penny, full price. Come on, let's go home. Even Clark Gable's not worth that much. "

"Mum, I'm paying. It's a pretty normal price. At Leicester Square you can pay a tenner."

We get into the auditorium, Dot grumbling continuously, then she wonders why "it's shrunk." I explain as best I can about multiplexes with their myriad screens. All around us, loopy old ladies are rustling bags, clanging mobility frames, dropping walking sticks and shaking umbrellas. The start of the film has no effect on the hubbub. Vivian Leigh's appearance gets them cooing, and there is a long and loud discourse somewhere to our left about whether she was 'common' or not. Clark Gable's arrival provokes plenty of oohs and aahs. A momentary hush during the first kiss between Scarlett and Rhett is disturbed by the high-pitched whine of a hearing aid in the row behind. At the end Dot's teary eyes are squinting at the credits, and even though I was bored witless by this never-ending melodrama I can see she's enjoyed herself.

"Clark Gable reminds me of your father, you know."

"Come on, Mum," I reply. "They're completely different. Dad was 5'4" in his boots, built like a whippet, and had thinning mousy hair."

"Ah, but you see Geoffrey's moustache was exactly the same as Clark Gable's. And he had the same dark eyes."

Reluctant to challenge these mixed-up memories any further, I let her witter on aimlessly until I'd got her home.

Elevenses: Fine tea of victoria sponge, rich tea and biscuits, almost made up for the tedium of the cinema. Then the bombshell: "Bernard, dear. That was really nice. I was thinking of going every week, if you would accompany me. There's *Mrs Miniver* next and *The Sound of Music* in a fortnight."

Oh Lord, just shoot me now and get it over with.

Wednesday 4th May: Spirals at Spirent AGM

Never thought I'd turn into one of those old buffers who turns up at shareholders meetings for the sandwiches and vol-au-vents. Still, hoped to find out what Spirent does and why I've lost so much. Didn't understand a word of the annual report. In my day, state of the art telecommunication testing meant picking up the receiver and barking down the Bakelite and seeing if you got an echo.

Never thought I'd miss the scrape of the train as it chugged across Hungerford Bridge on those misty mornings, hearing it again today, I found I did. Help!

Elevenses: A Twix on the train. Bit naughty.

Close of play: Portfolio up £136.20. Spirent rose after the chairman's statement. Maybe I'll just hang on.

Friday 10th June: Hobnobbing again

A better day. Jarvis crept up 4p! Clutching at straws perhaps, but maybe the recovery has began. Two years ago 4p was neither here nor there, but now here I am celebrating each and every twitch in the price. Surely someone wants to take it over. Please, please. Can't bear to take a six quid per share loss. Really can't.

Elevenses: Six Hobnobs…oh dear. Finished the packet. Eunice will find out. Can't bear another of those interrogations about cholesterol. The woman won't be happy until I'm eating Ryvita or some other Scandinavian hardboard and my insides are as dry and dusty as a Jewson's warehouse. Nipped out to Kwik Save to buy another packet of Hobnobs, hid all but six in the Hornby drawer, the balance going back in the biscuit tin. Cunning! That'll give me some respite for a few days.

Close of play: Portfolio up £18.62. Hooray!

Sunday June 12th: Incandescent about split-caps

The papers are saying that only those with zero dividend preference shares will get a bite at the split-cap compensation package. What about those of us with income shares, eh? Aren't we entitled to a bite of the compensation cake? I would have chosen zeroes if I'd known, but you don't normally start looking up who stands where in the creditors' queue when you buy an investment, do you? It would be like celebrating a christening by measuring the child for a coffin.

Elevenses: Half a crushed tube of Smarties that I found in the pocket of my overalls. Don't think I'd even worn them since February when the bathroom gutter fell off. Still, presume there's no sell-by date on such confections.

Eunice has been flicking through conservatory catalogues again. Though she's not said a word after our last bust-up on the issue, one brochure, with price tags that reach well into six figures, has been left very prominently in the den. She's as subtle as a hailstorm of anvils. The woman believes money grows on trees. If she'd worked or even contributed a penny in National Insurance in her life we wouldn't be so badly off, but now it's the usual refrain: "But Darling, you were supposed to support me. Thick and thin, don't you remember?"

Thursday 7th July: Bridging the divide

Finally finished my application form for split cap compensation. The deadline is in a week, and I've no idea how much if anything I will get. I was advised to buy the damn things by a commission-and-gin fuelled stockbroker, now resident in Ibiza and beyond the reach of (affordable) law. I was clearly mis-sold. That'll teach me to listen to Eunice's bridge partners, won't it?

Elevenses: Half a packet of jaffa cakes (delicious).

Close of Play: Share market up, Bernard's shares down.

Just mulling this repetitive misery when Eunice swans into the den, does a twirl and says: "So what do you think?"

Baffled by this prompt, I make a stab at it. "Oh, that's lovely. Mauve does really suit you. Nice buttons as well. Nice, very nice."

"Not the *cardigan*, Bernard," Eunice says testily. "How can you think I just bought this cardigan when you know perfectly well that *you* bought it for my birthday in 2003. You are hopeless, really."

"Ah yes, of course. The boots then?"

"Don't be dim, I bought those in Herne Bay last October. You must remember, while we visited Felicity? After her varicose vein operation, remember?"

"I really have no idea…"

"Look," she flicked at her hair. "Can't you see it's different?"

"Um…"

"Bernard, the highlights. And it's layered, now isn't it? It used to come straight down here at the back. Mr Paul says I have hair that's just brimming with thickness and vitality for a woman of my age."

"Mr Paul? Is that the hairdresser?"

"Principal stylist, Bernard. Catwalk Cuts doesn't employ 'hairdressers'. They have designers and stylists."

"And prices that would make a supermodel wince, no doubt."

"Bernard, if you had your way you'd have me queuing with the pensioners for the Wednesday morning £3.95 discount cut at Scissors, wouldn't you? Don't you think I'm worth more?"

Well, she certainly thinks she is. But it's muggins here who picks up the bill.

Monday 1st August: Peter's perfect portfolio

Had Peter and Geraldine over for dinner on Saturday. Peter Edgington and his oh-so-bloody-perfect portfolio. How can a man with holdings in three banks, a power generator and one oil and gas firm (BG Group) have done so well? The year's far from over and he's already made 18 per cent, twice what the FTSE has done. Besides, about half his money is in gilts and cash. I'm fully invested in shares, but I'm down. It just doesn't make sense. Naturally, Peter has just installed a hardwood framed conservatory ("none of this UPVC rubbish") and Eunice is absolutely green. Does he know that our entire house is framed in UPVC?

Elevenses: Three hobnobs from the secret stash. Very restrained.

Bought 1,000 shares in Lloyds TSB, ready for that big interim dividend later this month. What's good enough for Peter Perfect is good enough for me. I'll sell them as soon as I've got the payout.

Close of play: Portfolio down £170, Jarvis down again. Stand exactly where I was back in February. Tut, why do I bother?

Tuesday 9th August: Public spectacle

Lost my reading glasses for about three hours this morning. Hunted all over the house for them, in the loft, behind the PC. Got more and more irritable about it, especially when Eunice started to 'help'.

"Where did you last see them, Bernard?"

"I can't even tell you when I last saw through them."

"Alright, what was the last thing you read?"

"Um. That old Chronic Investor magazine that's in the en-suite."

"So did you leave your specs in the loo then?"

"Not that I could see. But that's the point, I need to be wearing the buggers to look for them."

At this point Eunice went off to search both bathrooms. "No, they're not there, but neither is the magazine."

"So?"

"So, Bernard, wherever you put the magazine down is probably where your specs are, yes?"

"Well, possibly."

"If you got yourself some varifocals like I suggested, you wouldn't need to take them off."

"Have you seen the price of varifocals? I don't really need the distance vision bit, it would be a waste of hundreds of pounds and Dolland & Aitchison would be rubbing their hands with glee."

"Well, what about half-moons then."

"Oh, come on. They make me look like a grandfather."

"Bernard, you *are* a grandfather."

"Yes, but I don't feel like one and I don't want to look like one."

"Well what is the alternative? You won't let me put a cord on them because you whinge that you look like a librarian. I give up."

Elevenses: Gave up on the specs, settled down for a Club Biscuit and a cuppa in the front room. As I plonked myself down I felt a crunch under my right buttock. Delving in the back pocket of my moleskins, I fished out the elusive spectacles, minus the left lens that had popped out. So that's another £5.99 down the drain.

Close of play: Up £183.60, so long as I count that Lloyds TSB dividend that I'll be entitled to tomorrow.

Wednesday 10th August: Paying dividends

Plagued by nuisance fax calls while I was waiting for daughter Jemima to ring me from the airport. Every minute the phone rang, and the moment I picked it up it just went 'beep' into my ear. Hung up, then exactly the same bloody thing happened one minute later. So I dialled 1471 to discover that the caller had "withheld their number". I wish I could withhold mine! I rang BT's nuisance call section, which apparently staffed with imbeciles and cretins.

No, it didn't count as a nuisance call. No, they couldn't tell me what number it came from. Well, yes if it was a breather they'd find out, but not for this. Then they suggested I should disconnect the phone for an hour! Idiots! I think I'll set up some fax calls to them, see how they like it.

Close of play: Down £215.30. Was going to sell Lloyds TSB, but the shares dropped so much now they're ex-dividend I'd actually be worse off. Must pay more attention to these things.

Chapter Two

Book Fair at St. Simeon's

Saturday 13th August: Crackerjack pencil

Eunice persuaded me to come with her to church for their annual book fair to raise money for the orphans of Kigali. This isn't our local C of E of course. St. Dunstan's isn't good enough for her and the five minute walk would mean few excuses not to go every Sunday. St. Simeon's is a good half hour drive but it has some rather worldly attractions apart from its fine Norman tower and crumbling honey stone masonry. Many of the local great and the good are found there, drawn from the large mock-Tudor houses which back on to the golf course. Eunice and her appallingly snobby crony Daphne Hanson-Hart go to church not to cleanse their souls and commune with God, but to elbow each other and hiss over the hymn books every time they spot a celebrity. Sometimes it's Lady Topham, and occasionally the Hon. Sir Giles Topham MP too. More usually there are the collection of 'formers': The former Blue Peter presenter, the former make-up woman for Kiki Dee and the former model wife of someone in

Eighties pop group Take This. Or do I mean Take That? Something do with punch-ups, anyway.

In glorious weather, the Reverend Alec McKenzie, who reputedly has part of the creed tattooed on one shoulder, is in fine, very camp, form. His retinue of adoring spinsters have set up three dozen trestle tables, heavy with bodice-rippers, forgotten poetry and Macedonian dentistry manuals, but so far there are few takers. I have just found myself a dog-eared but extensive collection of *Railway Modeller* when suddenly the sky turns as livid as a bruise and big fat raindrops start to ping down onto the tea urn beside me. With thousands of books primed for a soaking, the Rev. tries all he can to stop the punters fleeing for their BMWs. He rushes around, handing out Tesco bags yelling: "Fill a bag with books for a pound."

At the mention of such a discount, Eunice, who had been deep in conversation to Daphne about the evil of wheelie bins (which are soon to be introduced locally), suddenly finds passion for the plight of the orphans of Kigali and wades into the fray. Fifteen minutes later and out of breath, Eunice and I sit in the Volvo with the rain pounding on the roof and compare our purchases. Amongst many others I've got *101 Uses for a Dead Cat*, Harrap's *Dictionary of Ottoman Architecture*, a rather soggy 1967-71 collection of *Railway Modeller* and the 1963 *Airfix Annual*. She's got two bulging bags of Danielle Steele, a Maeve Binchy omnibus, *Rosemary Conley's Hip and Thigh Diet*, *Baskets! A celebration in Hazel, Willow and Raffia*, and finally (and most ominously) *Multi-Orgasmic after Menopause: A Guide for Couples with an introduction by Claire Rayner*.

"Single ones not good enough for you?" I ask, foolishly.

"They would be, Bernard. But I can't remember the last time..."

"Look," I say, pointing out through the rain-misted windscreen. "Isn't that the fellow who was on Crackerjack?"

"You mean Peter Glaze? No, I believe he died. And you're changing the subject."

"What subject?"

"Our love life. Or to put it another way, the infrequency of your wielding the Crackerjack pencil."

Elevenses: A delicious slice of victoria sponge, 85p from the Mothers Union stall. Rest of the day spent up in the loft with my locomotives hiding from Eunice and her darker motives.

Wednesday 31st August: Hurricanes galore

Saw news about Hurricane Katrina. All those homeless people, all that devastation. Bad taste thought (why is investment so full of them?) but perhaps it's high time to buy some oil shares. Probably should have bought them earlier in the year, and listened to Mike Delaney when he said Shell was a bargain. Still, never trust a man who wears corduroy, that my motto. Mike is covered in so much of the stuff that he gets snagged on the flock wallpaper in the curry house.

Shell or BP, Shell or BP, Shell or BP? Can't decide.

Elevenses: Slice of illicit Battenburg. Divine!

Close of play: Up £12.62. Notice Lloyds TSB starting to recoup the dividend. The penny's dropped about how ex-dividends work.

Tuesday 6ᵗʰ September: The quote arrives

Oil price still rising, and rigs are damaged in the Gulf of Mexico. Still can't decide what to buy. Found what appeared to be two corduroy hand grenades in the Hornby drawer. On closer inspection turned out to be kiwi fruit! What on earth Eunice expects me to do with those I can't imagine. Perhaps I'll pull the pins out and fling them at Hermès if she gets into the veg patch again.

3.30pm. The Conservatory quote has arrived! £43,200....Plus bloody VAT! I'll have to say no, I really will. That's more than half the value of the portfolio. I don't think she realises we haven't been making money. You can't fund that kind of outlay when you've just been treading water.

Elevenses: Battenburg crumbs, plus a mid-afternoon Islay to recover from the shock of that bill. Back's playing up now. Perhaps it's twinge drinking?

Close of play: Down £215.30. Jarvis weaker again, ho-hum. I really should sell.

Thursday 29ᵗʰ September: Porridge portfolio

Portfolio looks like porridge again. Third profit warning this month, this time from Compass. What's so difficult about serving up school dinners and squaddie meals? Bought the shares at 345p back in 2004, and now look at them. Not much more than two quid's worth. About enough to buy a coffee at Starbucks. Speaking of which…

Elevenses: Two eccles cakes and a cappuccino.

Bought 100 shares in First Choice Holidays after a tip in the Sunday papers, cost me £200. Paid for it by dumping my holdings in Shire Pharmaceuticals, which after a whole month seem to be going nowhere. At least I didn't lose anything except the £20 commission each side, and the stamp duty of course.

Close of play: Portfolio down £486.30. That's £900 down for the week so far. So that's the end of Eunice's conservatory plans, because I absolutely refuse to add it to the mortgage. Still, I'll be in trouble when I break the news to her.

Tuesday 4th October: Intruders in the Hornby drawer!

Mighty row about the conservatory yesterday evening. Eunice seems to think we need something the size of Brighton Pavilion attached to the back of the house. Went to find my biscuit stash this morning and guess what? Between the double-O gauge Spanish locomotive and the rare boxed Russian artillery wagon (what a find that was!) sat a giant packet of chocolate digestives which I had not put there. This must be an apology for calling me a "complete waste of space." Frankly it's the conservatory that will be a waste of space. It'll be filled up in a jiffy with second hand cane furniture, raffia baskets, and bloody toby jugs. Still, she seems as immovable on this subject as on any other.

Elevenses: Four chocolate digestives.

Close of play: Portfolio down £273.25 Bah humbug!

Saturday 8th October: Peter's boasting

Popped around to Peter and Geraldine's for coffee. While Eunice and Geraldine discuss HRT, (sounds like another new tax from Gordon Brown!) Peter all too happy to spirit me off to his appallingly tidy office and boast about what he's been investing in. Says he uses an automatic spreadsheet where the closing prices are automatically filled in. That's just flash, frankly. I prefer fiddling with my old bits of MoD graph paper. He just bought 15,000 BP shares at 640p, which he reckons is a bargain. But the *size* of the deal, 15,000 times £6.40! That must be worth…um, lots. Saw a cutting on his desk about a few recommended AIM companies. Think I might look that up when I get home.

Wednesday 19th October: Simple Simon says

Told Eunice about the 'portfolio situation'. Her reply?

"Oh Bernard, you spend simply hours in there hunched over that screen, surrounded by a sea of filthy crumbs and wearing that ragged old cardigan, and now you tell me we're losing money. What's it all been for?"

Then, the final insult: "Bernard, darling, why don't you just buy what Peter bought. He's made simply pots."

Because, you silly fool, he's already made the money. If I buy now, it's going to be too late. What I need to buy is what Peter will buy tomorrow not what he bought yesterday.

Elevenses: A whole packet of delicious high fat Scottish shortbread. See if I care!

Close of play: Too angry to look.

Friday 21st October: Wall Street beckons

My broker's website says I can now buy U.S. shares through them. Think I might start trading on Wall Street. Got my green eye shade and a nice Havana, what more do I need? Keep reading about Intel and those famously shrinking microchips which power the world's computers. Reminds me of my own investments: Bernard Jones and his incredible shrivelling investments. Or, a horror film for Eunice: *Honey, I shrunk the kids' inheritance.*

Read that millions of ordinary American's trade Intel. Seeing as half of them can't spell the name of their own country, there must be room for someone with a bit of breeding to turn an honest penny. Evening trading in the New York time zone would make a nice change from listening to Eunice snoring her way through Taggart.

Elevenses: The digestives have mysteriously vanished. Found one measly soft fig roll at the back of the Hornby drawer. Eunice has started leaving fruit for me again. I really do wish she'd stay out of the den.

Close of play: Up £8.03. Every little helps.

Monday 24th October: vindication

Oil price is falling again and so is BP's share price. Glad I didn't buy any at the time of Katrina! Must work out what Peter Perfect has lost. That's 15,000 times 34p, which must be five grand surely. Haha! Hornby, meanwhile is chugging ahead. It may be a small investment, but it's heading in the right direction. Finally decided to sell Jarvis. Good riddance, I say. Proceeds should buy a couple of windows in Eunice's palace, at least.

Elevenses: One and a half eccles cakes, the remainder having exploded in my hand. Took 20 minutes to get all the choux pastry out of the keyboard.

Close of play: Up £141.89.

Saturday 5th November: Bonfire of the sanities

For weeks now, we've had firework lunacy. Despite the new regulations, kids from the council estate have continued to get hold of bangers which they lob at old ladies in the high street, and every night until 2am we've endured sporadic booms that makes us feel like we live in Beirut. Then today, on the very day that there is supposed to be a proper public display, the council officials decide after a last minute inspection that the local Round Table cannot after all use Densley Fields as they have for 20-odd years because "access for emergency vehicles is inadequate". How ridiculous! What a nation of killjoys we've become.

Elevenses: A Club Biscuit. What sad emasculated things these have become. Time was when a Club was so thickly coated, you could nibble the chocolate off all round in big chunks. Now it's thinner than an undertaker's smile.

Sunday 6th November: Research department

Decided to have a bit of a root and branch rethink on the investment front. Ploughed through a stash of old investment magazines, found a useful piece on price earnings ratios and why they matter. Maybe I'm in above my head, seeing as I don't know a P&L from a G&T or (S&M for that matter). Found an article about defence companies. At least I know all about these fellas. Got a lifetime's MoD knowledge I should put to good use.

Elevenses: Packet of crisps, allegedly smoky beef with wholegrain mustard. Tasted more like char-grilled linoleum. How do they name these flavours? Presumably someone makes a mistake on the smoky bacon line, tips in a tonne too much acidity regulator or locust bean gum or whatever, and the supervisors stand around munching on them like Jilly Goolden: "I'm getting sun-dried tomatoes, drizzled with olive oil…"

Must make sure Eunice doesn't find the empty crisp packet which is still in my blazer pocket.

Tuesday 6th December: Inspiration and discipline

Decided on an investment diet: Buy nothing above a P/E of 10 or a dividend yield below what I get on my savings account (3 per cent). If it's cheap it shouldn't fall, and at least I'll get as much in income as if I'd taken Eunice's advice and stuck it all in the bank. Better still, maybe I will stick it in a bank. I've paid enough in bloody bank charges over the years. Now, which of them is best?

Used the stock screener that Peter Edgington showed me, and got a list of 20 companies with a P/E below 10 and a 3 per cent or better yield.

Elevenses: Nothing, got doctor's appointment today. Quack's bound to give me grief on the biscuit front.

Close of play: Down £12.53.

Christmas Eve 2005: Cutting down the costs

Changes to the portfolio are all doing well. Dominos Pizza is up 7 per cent in a few weeks, BAe likewise. Decided to keep the Lloyds TSB instead of chucking it out, and I'm thinking about Scottish Power now that the Germans have flounced off when they're bid was rejected. Also, finally decided to move to a proper online broker. Found one that only charges ten quid a trade! I had no idea you could get it so cheap. Worked out I could have saved hundreds this year. Of course I'd have saved even more if I hadn't traded at all! New year resolutions are next to be worked on. I'm going to make this the last year that I lose money.

Chapter Three

Yuletide Misery

Christmas Day: Buzzards and sporrans

Whole family round for a bellicose Christmas of braying inanities, pointless rows and indigestion while slumped in front of the Sound of Music. After last year's food poisoning incident, Eunice has at least given up the free range organic buzzards, or whatever species that mottled monster was. The Volvo's boot still stinks of it. Buying from local farms is all very well, but give me a Waitrose turkey crown any day. While Tesco has become the big bad wolf, Waitrose is like the Queen, no-one has an unkind word to say. Shame you can't buy shares in it, but perhaps that's the point. A jolly worker's cooperative without the hammer and sickle. There aren't many places where both Eunice's vegan friend Irmgard and Monday Club members like the Hon. Giles Topham MP would both be happy to be seen shopping.

Pressies were fair to middling. I had fantasised about the Hornby live steam LNER Flying Scotsman with double tender, but at £525 that was never going to happen. Perhaps if I sell the shares in Hornby, then I can almost afford one! The Smoky Joe Caledonian Railways saddle tank loco was an imaginative second best at thirty quid (Thank you, Brian and Janet), though *clearly* as my only son Brian should realise it doesn't fit with a 1930s Great Western layout.

Eunice also bought me a book about Warren Buffett, called *The Midas Touch*. Could certainly do with a little of that. Everything I invest in turns not into gold but into a different four-letter word.. I'll certainly need to be like the Sage of Omaha now that we've arranged to stick the cost of the conservatory on the mortgage. Why do I never win these fights? The new space will get cluttered up with china knick-knacks and cat litter just like the existing rooms.

As for those M&S tartan boxer shorts, that's daughters for you. Jemima has had 27 years to realise I'm a Y-fronts man. I hold Stuart Rose personally responsible for that three-pack of billowing kilts. If this is their idea of the products to turn the company round, the only way to do it is by using them as sails. Still, at least M&S allow you to change them without the receipt.

Boxing Day : Seconds out, round two

Most of the clan has departed. Just Brian and Janet left, and everyone's favourite little Antichrist, Digby. Still only seven, the monster grandson refuses to eat anything except baked beans, spaghetti hoops and Dairylea cheeses, all with lashings of salad cream. The tantrums are unbelievable. Of course this has been clear from birth. I knew he was going to be a bad one when he vomited into my ear while I held him at the christening. I couldn't hear properly for weeks.

By 3pm I was able to escape into the den to look at Wall Street prices. What workaholics those Yanks are, even trading on Boxing Day. Have decided I will definitely open a spread-betting account. Making more with less seems the way to go.

Tuesday 27th December : Salad cream days

Got my application off, all online and very simple. None of that nonsense about sending in copies of utility bills or passports like you do for a bank or stockbroking account. Paused slightly at the warning about the danger of possibly losing more than you invest. Sounds a bit like negative equity to me. Still, nothing to worry about. You just wait until the situation improves, like Eunice and I did with the house in Guildford Road in the early nineties. Shouldn't be a problem.

4.30pm: Brian and Janet are still here, and the creature from the black lagoon is driving us mad. Had to nip out to Kwik Save for another bottle of salad cream (Eunice's home-made egg mayonnaise clearly isn't good enough for the little tyke), which at least gave me the opportunity to slyly take advantage of a two-for-one offer on Cadbury's mini rolls. These now reside undiscovered in the depths of the Hornby drawer. Have a copy of the Cadbury annual report somewhere, must take a peek sometime.

Wednesday 28th December : The trend is your friend

Snowed today! A good couple of inches dusting the woods and paddock behind. Looks delightful. Made my first spread bet, a £2 per point up bet on the FTSE. Made £34 in fifteen minutes! This looks easy. Just wait to see which way the market is moving, and go with the flow. Feeling indulgent towards the world in general, I suggest to Digby that a snowman would be a good idea. His usually sullen face widens into a huge grin.

"Yeah, cool!" he coos. "Can we get it from the garden centre? They have huge ones," he said stretching his arms wide. Slowly it dawns on me. He wants one of those ghastly inflatable jobs from the Wyevale, as featured atop porches in the council estate! No, I say. We're going to *make* one.

"Uh?" he yells. My God, whatever happened to childhood! Has the boy never played with snow?

"He gets chilled easily, Bernard," Janet warns as she wraps the urchin up in fifteen layers of multi-coloured woollens, blue-spotted Wellingtons and a voluminous anorak that wouldn't have disgraced Scott of the Antarctic. "We're just going outside, we may be some time," say I, as we exit. Of course, the child complains that the snow is cold and after five minutes wants to go in. So I end up making the snowman on my own, rolling a great squeaking ball of ice around the lawn while my son, daughter-in-law and their vermin offspring watch from the house. I almost give myself a hernia lifting it upright and placing a second ball of snow on top. My old pipe, two lumps of anthracite and a Dairylea cheese for the nose complete the picture.

Had just come in when Eunice hissed at me "Bernard, I thought you might like to know that Brian has taken Digby upstairs to play with your train set."

Aargh! I flew upstairs, snowy wellies and all, banging my elbow on the banister. Too late, they are already up in the loft and the Antichrist is making chuffing noises as he tries to *push* my Devon Belle Pullman locomotive!

"Why don't the wheels go round, Dad?" says Brian. Through gritted teeth I carefully explain about precision electric motors for the umpteenth time, emphasising that a model railway is not the same as a train set. Not a toy. Do all school teachers lack common sense, or merely the one I sired? Then I notice that there is salad cream grease on the loco, and the points and the switches. Brian, watching my face, tries wiping it off with his sleeve. Digby, of course, is grinning like a loon. I give up, I really do. Still, only one more day to go and they depart.

Thursday 29th December: Bovis and Butthead

Brian, in earnest schoolmaster mode, is lecturing us over the final lunch about the way housebuilders are despoiling the countryside. There's some giant new estate planned over the back of their home, and having bombarded the council with objections they have got precisely nowhere. The plans are for affordable homes based on a masterplan drawn up by John Prescott, but that presumably doesn't count the insurance premiums seeings as most of the site is in a flood plain.

Having bought 500 shares in Bovis before Christmas, I'm feeling a little defensive though God knows a few hundred pounds profit is a rare enough event. Little Barratt boxes, he says, ruining our green and pleasant land, and *you're* helping finance them. But what about the schoolteachers and the nurses, I say, where are they going to live without affordable housing? Not everyone has the help you did from us, Brian. Janet's expression shows that is a low blow, and I suppose I should regret it. But he does come out with such tosh. Britain's housebuilders are merely following government rules to make the best use of land. In any case it isn't green and pleasant. It is brownfield, old quarries, railway sidings and weed-strewn tips in places like Slough and Harlow.

Elevenses: Two mini-rolls. Three others, however, are missing. I suspect Digby, and the brown smears around his maw seem proof positive, but seeing as Eunice doesn't know about them I just glare at him and keep schtum. I sense something rather too clever about that child. He has an unerring sense of what he can get away with filching. Right from the start I had my doubts about him. He was due to be born breech-first in traditional Jones fashion, and resisted all attempts by the midwife to turn him, or indeed to be born at all. Thus, by caesarean section, was begun the Antichrist's first assault on the encompassing flesh of the world that nurtures him. Poor Janet has never been quite the same since.

Late in the afternoon, I return to the den to look at Wall Street. Out of the window I notice that the snowman has been kicked down. The pipe and coal are lying on the grass, but the Dairylea cheese has vanished.

Friday 30th December: Blessed peace

I celebrate the first family-free day for a week with a little up spread-bet on Nasdaq at £3 per point. Barely moves, so having stared at it until 9pm, I leave it to roll over into the New Year. Bit more boring than I thought. Still can't, expect markets to move all the time. Couldn't find the Cadbury-Schweppes annual report, so I trawled through the web site. Like others brought up on the stuff, I always thought Cadbury was synonymous with chocolate. I always forget about the drinks side. Now there's chewing gum too. I suppose that adds a bit of balance. When it's too hot for chocolate, they can sell more Dr Pepper, when its too cold for fizzy pop, they sell more chocolate. And chewing gum keeps the jaws going year round.

Amazed to discover they are planning to open a 'centre of excellence' in the U.S. for chewing gum 'innovation'. What tosh. Presumably that means ways to make it stick better on tube and bus seats, easier ways to flick it across the classroom, and enhanced gob-open chewing noises for chavs. Having seen what Cadbury is up to, I'm quite glad the shares are on an expensive P/E of 21 and yield only 2.7 per cent. Avoid, as they say in the investment mags.

Elevenses: Two mini-rolls and a cup of BournVita. I have now found the wrappers from those mini-rolls stolen by Digby, scrunched up and stuffed into the points of my model railway. This really is about three crimes in one, (including endangering the safety of the miniature travelling public) but I really can't say anything without getting into trouble with the cake constabulary.

Close of Play: Final day of the year, and the portfolio has recovered quite well. I'm only down 3% this year. Still, can hardly bear to measure myself against the FTSE 100 which is up over nearly 17 per cent.

New Year's Eve : Time for a fresh start

Round to the Edgingtons for one of their dreadful parties. *Auld Lang Syne*, sweet sherry, and crowding on the sofa next to incontinent great aunts. All the while other people on telly having fun, which we stare at until quarter past midnight when everyone demands to be driven home. Still, a new year is a new start. 2006 will be better after five miserable years of losses. When old investments be forgot, and never brought to mind. I'm going to make enough to pay off that damn conservatory by my birthday, if it kills me.

Chapter Four

Below the Belt

Tuesday 3ʳᵈ January: New Year, new chances
    First trading day of the New Year. January, they say, is the best month of the year in the stock market. Let's hope so. Since last Thursday I've had a £3 per point up-bet riding on the Nasdaq Composite Index on Wall Street, with a break-even of 2,223. Now, with Wall Street about to open, I'm down about a tenner but the pre-market reports say there could be an uplift. Trouble is, can't sit and watch the action this week. Eunice wants to drag me along to the sales, and (Oh God) we've got tea with my mother on Thursday.
    Elevenses: Slice of leftover Christmas dundee cake, smuggled out of the tin in the kitchen. If discovered will blame grandson who, as they say in the CID, has 'form'. Will keep the Hornby drawer empty of snacks for now seeing as Eunice seems to check it regularly.
    Close of Play: Nasdaq jumps to 2,244, which puts me sixty quid in the money!

Better still, Bovis continues to climb. I paid 590p in October and now they're nearly 800p, but still only on a P/E of 11.

Wednesday 4th January: The boxer rebellion

Being dragged around the sales by Eunice was bloody *awful*. Dismal weather, Bluewater crowded, traffic absolutely vile. To put a cherry on it, M&S wouldn't take the bloody tartan boxers back because Eunice let slip I'd tried one pair on. Only one pair, I ventured, why won't you take back the other two? Because they're sold as a set, that's why. The pretty young shop assistant gave me this withering look which said: Poor sod, now you've got to wear them.

Mike Delaney popped round after lunch, a vision in corduroy, dandruff and crepe-sole moccasins. Asked me whether I was interested in the investment club he was setting up, Wednesday lunchtimes in the back room at the Ring o'Bells. Sounds interesting, fits in with my New Year resolutions, except perhaps the one about booze. What *his* were, I dread to think. Clearly didn't include a sartorial rethink, nor stopping smoking. As he settled into the sofa and unpeeled a new packet of Lambert & Butler, Eunice noisily banged down a glass ashtray for him. Not a pause. Skin like a rhino, that man. Immediately, smoke drifts everywhere, because like Bill Clinton, he doesn't inhale. Unfortunately, as Eunice pointed out afterwards, our curtains, furniture, clothes and hair most certainly do inhale. Yes, yes, I agreed after she took me aside, I'll have a quiet word.

Elevenses: Another slice of illicit dundee cake. A rock-hard pear has mysteriously materialised in the Hornby drawer. It's Chinese, according to the label. Avoid at all costs.

Close of play: More progress on the Nasdaq. Yee-ha!

Thursday 5th January: Teatime torment

Mum, it has to be admitted, is a few unit trusts short of a portfolio. For Dorothy, then Dot, now at 89 clearly Dotty, every footstep is in a world long disappeared. She doesn't realise that memory lane was demolished to make way for the M25 twenty years ago. This time it's a lost purse crisis.

"Well, I had left it on the counter at that bank."

"Which one?"

"You know, next door to Joe Lyons."

"Mum, the corner house isn't there any more. The Luftwaffe destroyed it. Do you mean the Halifax?"

"…but this nice young man saw me and followed me past the Gaumont.."

I nodded. Yes, the Gaumont cinema built in about 1910, turned into a Locarno dance hall in 1956, into a bingo hall in 1977, into flats in 1993 or thereabouts, then gutted by fire last year.

Now it's a gaming arcade on the ground floor, and boarded up above. Fifty years of social history just passed her by.

"He finally caught up with me at Timothy White's."

"Boots, Mum."

"Well it always used to be Timothy White's."

"Until about 1970, yes. But he did give you the purse back?"

"Oh yes, ever so kind he was. All me tickets were still in it."

"You mean your Halifax card?"

"Anyway I give him a ten bob note for his trouble. He was pleased as punch."

"A ten bob note! Mum, what colour was it, orange or purplish?"

"Purple."

Eunice breaks in: "That was twenty *pounds*, Dot, not ten bob. They don't have ten bob notes anymore."

"Twenty pounds? It never was!" Mum looks shocked.

"Bernard, it's no good," whispers Eunice, when Mum is off making a cuppa. "She can't cope. I think she'll have to go into an H-O-M-E."

"I'm not going into a home," Mum yells from the kitchen. "And I'm not deaf. And I can still S-P-E-L-L." Then she comes in, all smiles.

"Mrs Oldroyd at number 14 is moving in with her son in March. He's ever such a good boy, always was."

Oh God!

Friday 6th January: Smalls and shorts

Doing a bit of research on M&S. Even setting aside the boxer rebellion, I was highly unimpressed by my last trip. Eunice, though admittedly no paragon of fashion, was underwhelmed too. If your matronly fifty-something won't buy the knitwear, who will? At 500p, the shares trade at 16 times forecast earnings, and have climbed absurdly seeing how much competition there is for dwindling consumer spending. Clearly a lot of investors *want* to see it do well. Perhaps this is a good contrarian opportunity to test the ability to short spread-bet. I'll take a look next week.

Elevenses: One Starburst. Thought I'd try these born-again Opal Fruits, but forgotten what sickeningly perfumed things they are. Threw the rest of the packet away. The Chinese pear, resolutely stone-like, squats inscrutably in the Hornby drawer.

Close of play: Up £145.

Monday 9th January: A quiet word

Mike Delaney came round again. This time the fag was already in his mouth before I'd opened the door, and I gagged from the first breath. He walked straight in, plonked himself down and asked whether I was up for the investment club. I hedged my affirmative until I knew who else was in. Mike's a nice enough fella (at a distance), but he loses money as readily as I do. On the other hand, while I want to glean some expert tips, I do not want some Peter bloody Edgington lecturing me. Mike said he's asked a few regulars at the Ring o'Bells, but there were no definites yet. That should rule Peter out. The Bells isn't one of his watering holes. Damn, forget to have that 'quiet word about smoking'.

Elevenses: Two fig rolls. The Chinese pear has gone from inedibly hard to inedibly rotten in just three days. Had probably sat in suspended animation in some chilled warehouse since the start of the T'ang dynasty.

Tuesday 10th January: Mum's the word

Mum's finances nagging at me. Drove around first thing, praying that she's not quite as broke as I fear. Relieved that her Halifax account still has a couple of grand in it, though she *will* keep drawing out huge wads of cash, leaving rolled notes in elastic bands in Aunty Vi's Burmese teapot, behind the cuckoo clock and (Lord preserve us) under the mattress. All the places even the dimmest drug-addled teenage burglar would guess. However, in a moment of clarity she digs out a vanity case from under the stairs, bulging with old papers. So I lug them home for a fuller investigation.

Elevenses: Mum at least knows what I like. Two slices of battenburg, an eccles cake and four chocolate fingers. "I shan't tell that woman," she promises, referring to Eunice whom she has never liked.

Close of play: Nasdaq teetering, so took profits at 2,320. Only deposited a grand in the spread-betting account, and that's nigh-on 300 smackers already! Still, get slightly depressed when I realise this covers only four ornate brass curtain poles on Eunice's conservatory.

Wednesday 11th January: Inequitable Life

Finally took a look at the great sheaf of Equitable Life stuff I received last year. To read it, you would never know what a disaster has occurred. I start ploughing through my notes, feeling the old blood pressure soaring again. Back in 2000 there was a too-and-fro in the courts about which particular Peter should be robbed to pay Paul, a graphic display of the disadvantages of a mutual. At least with a Plc, there's shareholder equity to raid. Instead it was guaranteed annuity rate customers against us, the poor with-profits wallahs. Law Lords backed the GAR people. So in 2001, I lost 16% of my policy straight off. Then in September 2001 they had the nerve to give me back 4% on condition I sign away rights to sue the management. Now I read that they still barely have a penny in equities! They missed out on a golden opportunity to recoup billions. Instead, by sticking everything in government bonds and cash which yielded bugger-all, they missed out on a share rally which from the low point of 2003 has pushed the FTSE 100 up 57%! That's not investment, it's perversity.

Elevenses: Three chocolate mini-rolls, munched absent-mindedly while perusing Equitable Life. Eunice 'had a word' about the disappearing dundee cake. "Bernard, you can't deny it. I lifted your keyboard and found sultanas there." Oh crumbs!

Chapter Five

Happy Discovery

Thursday 12th January: Hidden gold

Astonishing discovery! Digging through Mum's documents (mostly rubbish) came across three ancient share certificates, issued in Dad's name in 1936. One was for 75 shares in Gallaher, another was 1,780 in Anglo-Ecuadorian Oil, but here's the biggest find: 100,000 shares in English Electric Co. Ltd. It'll take some work to find out, but they could be worth a fortune. Good old Dot! She may be a barmy old hoarder, but that has its advantages.

Friday 13th January: Digging for victory

Lucky day for some! Am sitting here with a share certificate from 1936 that might be the saving of all our bacon. English Electric Co Ltd, 100,000 shares, in Dad's name, but it must have been Grandad's money because Dad would only have been 16. Nothing about it in the will. So what of English Electric? I know the company was a mainstay of British industry for half a century and I assume it merged or was taken over. Could it have gone bankrupt? I don't think so. Wanted to Google it this morning, but damn Internet connection went down. I could phone know-it-all Peter Edgington, but I'd rather he didn't know about this for now.

Got a cracking headache after yelling at BT about the Internet line. They're looking into it. Feeling a bit shivery too.

Elevenses: Two paracetamol and a Lemsip, then off to bed. Before I turned in, finally put in that short spread-bet on Marks & Spencer at 482p, by phone at £10 a point. That'll teach them to refuse to take back the boxers!

Thursday 19th January: Beating the system

Almost a week in bed with 'flu. Ghastly. Eunice has plied me with enough orange juice to upset the price of Florida citrus futures. The worst thing about being ill, is being powerless under the care regime: Kiwi fruit breakfasts, rock-hard wholemeal toast, aubergine and celeriac bake for lunch and endless 'mystery' soups, from the vegan cookery book Irmgard lent her. I'd kill for an eccles cake!

Waited until Eunice had set off to the chemist, and crawled down to the den. Hornby drawer has been ransacked, not a crumb remains. Desk wiped and polished and all my papers stacked in a heap. I'll never find anything now! Quick check online shows a) dial-up now works b) M&S is resolutely stable.

Elevenses: Desperate hunt for edibles. Cake's gone. Biscuit tin in kitchen empty, as per usual. Fridge stuffed full of green kryptonite, the vegetable that slayed Superman. It's cunningly labelled as curly kale, but I'm not fooled. While looking in lowest cupboards, saw something right at the back behind the pickle jars. A packet, stuck to the shelf. A good tug brings it away. Yes! It's a half packet of Penguins! Best before date illegible and, worryingly, looks to be in Aramaic. Gobble the lot down and scurry back to bed. Bliss!

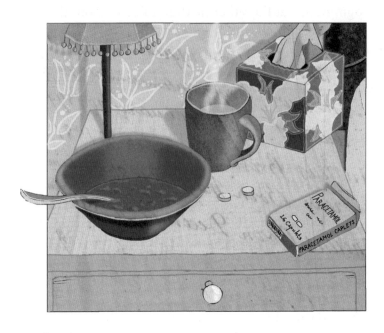

Friday 20th January: They're back

Seems now to be gastric 'flu. Awful, *awful* Hyderabad guts. I blame the curly kale. Mike Delaney phoned up about the share club, Eunice ran upstairs with the question. Yes, yes I said, count me in. Whatever, as they say in New York. Inaugural meeting February 1st. Then more ding-donging at the door. No peace, no sleep. Put pillow over head, feign death. Hear thundering up and down the stairs, banging bags and theatrical shushing. For God's sake! An hour later, when the hubbub is merely downstairs, I venture out on 14th trip to the loo.

The door to Jemima's old room is open. Oh Lord! They're back, tucked up along the edge of the pillow: Tiggy the Tiger, Jumbo Wiggy, Mrs Teasel the hedgehog, Mr Bear and assorted supporting characters. This can only mean one thing. My daughter, an allegedly high-flying international corporate lawyer of 27, has broken up with yet another chinless boyfriend, and has fled home. Sure enough I can hear plaintive sobs from downstairs. When I descend, I find that though it's gone midday I'm not the only one in pyjamas. Jemima, in heart-bedecked brushed cotton is draped around Eunice's neck, snivelling. For God's sake *grow up*!

Elevenses: Two Arret tablets and a glass of water. Delhi belly gone, but now suffering from Mysore bum.

Monday 23rd January: Toby or not Toby, that is the question

Feel somewhat better, though neglected. Jemima receiving oceans of Eunice's sympathy over Toby. Put up with my share of "Daddy, Daddy you're the only reliable man in the world," and the dreadful continental-style spontaneous hugging. Asked my opinion of Terrible Toby, I offer that there never seemed much to like or dislike, and indeed there wasn't. Tall, smartly dressed, well-polished shoes. Something in derivatives, polite but vacant. However, turns out to be gay, apparently. Foolishly ventured: "Can't be *that* gay, can he? You've been sharing a bedroom for 18 months". Eunice barked "Bernard!" at double the usual volume. Scuttled away to the den, to sift through Mum's papers, and dream about untold riches.

Elevenses: Tin of Heinz tomato soup. Finally, something even Eunice can't find fault with. One of the five-a-day portions, and it tastes nice too. If only we had some white bread for *proper* toast.

Close of play: Down £486 at one point, but market recovered almost all but a little. Thinking about that share certificate. Tomorrow, I'll find out for sure!

Chapter Six

The Curse of Marconi

Tuesday 24ᵗʰ January – Telent scout

Feeling much better. Up bright and early, and down into the den like a squirrel. Aha! Among Mum's papers is a yellowed page ripped out of the Times of December 9ᵗʰ 1936 giving the day's share bargains. English Electric changed hands at 27/9, presumably 27 shillings and nine pence, while Gallaher was around £6 (that's odd, because they're only a third higher now). But think, this certificate for English Electric alone was worth £127,000 back in 1936. It could be worth a million or more by now! Looked up English Electric on the web. I had thought it was taken over by Hawker Siddeley or BTR, but I was wrong. It was bought in 1968 by GEC, during Arnold Weinstock's day. Slight sense of foreboding because GEC became Marconi (one disaster I never partook of), so it won't have grown much in recent years. Found Marconi's website, and blow me down, they've changed their name *again*. This time to Telent. Pity the switchboard gals: "Hello, GEC..I mean Hello, Marconi, I mean Hello, Telent."

Phoned Telent, who said try the share registrars. Tried their number and after pressing lots of buttons got through. The name English Electric produced no recognition, neither did pre-war share certificates. They have nothing prior to 1980, suggested I try the company. "But I've tried them. They told me to call you!" Slammed the phone down in disgust.

Elevenses: Took a constitutional and nipped out to Kwik Save, while Eunice and Jem conduct a Toby post-mortem. Bought a Cadbury's Flake which I consumed en-route, and two packets of jaffa cakes for stashing away. Need somewhere safer that the Hornby drawer, unless I can find the key to lock it.

Close of trade: Quick glance showed Marks & Spencer absolutely unchanged at 482p from my short-sell price. Down, boy!

Wednesday 25th January: Sniffing out the truth

Made a cautious call to Peter Edgington, self-styled investment oracle. "How would you find the history of a company 30 or 40 years ago, if you can't get it online?" He suggested the company secretary, who have annual reports back to the year dot. If there was a company archivist, he said, they would know.

"Which company, Bernard?" he asked casually, the sly old dog. I fobbed him off, but I'm sure he will keep sniffing.

Jemima announced she was taking us out to dinner up in town. Eunice ordered me to dress up, so it was best blazer and brogues, and a quick blast with the nasal hair trimmer. Jem, appropriately enough in black, looked the professional lawyerette, a world away from the sullen child of recent days. Wonderful bottle of Chablis, superb sea bass, and best of all, traditional spotted dick and custard. No doubt a bill to match. Altogether an excellent evening until the last few minutes. Eunice went off to the ladies, and Jem says: "Daddy, don't like to ask, but I know what a share whizz you are. Thought you might have a spare twenty I could borrow?"

Baffled, because I had thought she was paying, I reach for my wallet.

"No, not for tonight. I've got that covered. No, I have a bit of a problem, because of Toby," she says.

As she gabbles out the dreary details, which she seemingly doesn't want Eunice to hear, it slowly dawns on me that her twenty isn't twenty pounds (or ten bob, like Mum thinks), it's twenty *thousand*. My daughter, casual as a cat, wants to borrow twenty *thousand* pounds. It's the invisible word, like a stealth bomber in the middle of the phrase, that causes the damage. I'm too stunned to reply, and Eunice is soon back, sniffing conspiracy.

"What are you two up to?"

I fumble for a reply: "I've decided that we shall treat Jem tonight. Isn't it good to have her back?".

Thursday 26ᵗʰ January: Hippopotamus manoeuvres

Eunice, decidedly squiffy after five glasses of wine, inflicted a hippopotamus manoeuvre on me last night. Cleaning my teeth, and still reeling from Jem's loan request, I didn't notice she had donned the dreaded black negligeé. Seeing my expression as I emerged from the en-suite, she adopted a wounded tone.

"Bernard, please show *willing* tonight. We've done nothing since Boxing Day morning." So the old soldier, eventually standing to attention, was led to his duty.

Tricky time coming up, a veritable minefield for hippo ambushes: January 30ᵗʰ (Our anniversary), February 4ᵗʰ (Her birthday), February 14ᵗʰ (An inevitability, this one) then April 1ˢᵗ (My birthday, but I'm expected to want some). In this struggle, my ammo box of excuses is even lower than my libido. Lumbago (over-used), headaches (too predicable), tiredness (pathetic, really). Too much alcohol. (v. high risk: It works on me, but makes Eunice utterly carnivorous). Blood pressure tablets might be promising though. Better still, perhaps I should do a Toby and claim I'm gay.

Friday 27th January: Home, home on the range

Finally got through to someone in Telent's (i.e. Marconi) company secretary department at 3pm. V. helpful woman. Seems GEC takeover of English Electric in 1968 was of five GEC ordinary shares for every three English Electric ordinary, which means Dad's 100,000 shares equate to 166,666 GEC shares. Then there was a 2:1 split in 1982, making the total 333,332. She looked in the 1999 annual report and said GEC was then worth £5.77 a share. Good God, that's nearly £2m! Surely even Marconi couldn't have put paid to all that! She said the recapitalisations of Marconi in 2003 were complex, and there was something about British Aerospace too, so she would e-mail the details. Cloud Nine!!

Eunice is taking Jem to the cinema with Irmgard and numerous trendy cronies tonight. Going to see *Bentback Mountain*, or whatever it's called . What *is it* about middle-aged women and woofters? Eunice never showed the slightest bit of interest in Audie Murphy, Alan Ladd or Bonanza. I can only assume that seeing naked chaps, or even chaps wearing chaps, tickles her. There was some resentment that I refused to go. "Bernard, you have no tenderness. To you the word tender means something that trundles behind a locomotive." Well, I retorted, I hope you show the same enthusiasm to accompany *me* when the lesbian stage version of the *Sound of Music* comes to the West End.

Elevenses: Two undercover jaffa cakes, packets now secreted in the long tunnel on the railway layout. She'll never find them. Got an appointment with the quack first thing on Monday. Not looking forward to that.

Monday 30th January : Returning to the nest

Got through last night's wedding anniversary celebration (our 38th) unscathed on the hippopotamus front. Low key meal with Eunice at the Harrow, then sat up talking to Jem until the small hours about debts. By the time I went up Eunice was fast asleep, apparently gargling in Flemish.

The Jem situation is dire. She and Toby bought an expensive flat in Fulham 18 months ago. He's given up his job and gone off to Costa Rica with a saxophone-playing bond salesman called Carlos. Toby used to pay the whole mortgage, but isn't paying anything now.

Jem reckoned she had a solution: "Now I do understand you haven't got the twenty to spare Daddy, so I was thinking that I can just keep it together with the mortgage and the credit card debts so long as I don't have any other costs, apart from getting the train in to work."

"Are you hinting you want to move back in?"

"Oh Daddy! You're so sweet. That be OK, wouldn't it? If you just rent a van and help me shift all my clutter back here, then I can rent the flat out. Simple!"

What could I say? At least now Eunice's giant conservatory will be used, if nothing else, to house Jemima's Hamley's-sized soft toy collection.

Elevenses: A Crunchie on the way back from the Quack's. Had samples of everything from blood to urine taken and tested. Blood pressure too high. Lots of impertinent questions about diet and alcohol from some humourless locum young enough to be my son. Lectures on exercise and cholesterol. Have to phone for results in a day or two. Not looking forward to that.

Close of play: Bovis still doing well. No sign of that Telent e-mail. Come on, come on!

Tuesday 31st January: Shareholder value

Absolutely scandalous! Unbelievable! Got the Marconi e-mail. Much worse than I thought, with two recapitalisations in 2003. In the first, for every 559 old Marconi shares, you get one new share plus something called warrants. So that's 333,334 divided by 559, which my lying Woolworth's calculator insists is 596. Check it and re-check, knock it on the wall, but that's it. Then in the second in July 2003, for every five shares, *again* you get just one, which makes that certificate worth 119 Telent shares. And what are they trading at? I look up in the Telegraph, a shade under £4. So a shareholding that was worth £136,000 in 1936, and £1.9m in 1999 is now reduced to just £476. Am absolutely incandescent with rage, and storm out for a walk.

Elevenses: An entire packet of four fondant fancies from Kwik Save, mostly consumed NAAFI style while in the interminable checkout queue. Checkout girl looks up after running the empty box over the barcode reader, to see my hamster-like cheeks bulging. I gave her the cash and fled. Still haven't got Eunice a birthday present. Damn.

Close of play: Didn't look. Can't bear to see another share price today. I feel like giving up. How is it that a managerial disaster at a company I had the good sense never to invest in can still be our ruination?

Friday 3rd February: Cholesterol capers

Awkward day. Marks & Spencer shares continue to climb, however much I stare at the screen and will them to self-destruct. At 499p, my inaugural spread-bet short-sell is now 17p in the red, that's £170. Still, I'm pretty sure that 500p will be barrier too far. Meanwhile, Eunice badgered me relentlessly all morning to phoned the quack's for the results of Monday's medical. While I made the call, she lurked nearby like a hyena sniffing wounded prey. As expected: Cholesterol too high. Blah-blah. Make new appointment. Discuss diet. "Oh good, that's a relief then," I said to the nurse as I put the phone down. Told Eunice everything was fine. Her narrowed eyes indicate scepticism. I'll hear more about this for certain.

Elevenses: Last two jaffa cakes from the long tunnel.

Close of play: Hornby shares have been climbing sharply since a trading statement on Monday which reckoned the railway modelling enthusiast is alive and well. I am now! The price has steamed up 30 per cent from 170p to 220p. Still, it is a shame the company seems to be shunting all production across to China.

4.50pm: Oh God! Still haven't got Eunice a birthday present. It's tomorrow! Tore into town, got stuck in rush hour traffic as shops gradually emptied and closed. Finally parked and found I'd left my damn list and reading glasses behind. This is going to be a disaster!

Saturday 4th February: Gift horses examined

"A Homer Simpson mug tree, Bernard. How nice." Eunice distinctly cool about her presents. Did little better with the Victorian-style pyjamas, even though (amazingly) they were the right size. I thought she'd appreciate M&S's evocation of the industrial designs of Isambard Kingdom Brunel lovingly recaptured in rivet-pleated, reinforced winceyette. As for Nigella Lawson's *How to be a Domestic Goddess* Eunice muttered that when I became a domestic god, she would up her game, and not before.

Elevenses: Had to play host to Eunice and her cronies for unbelievably tedious birthday coffee and biscuits. Irmgard, the spaniel-faced vegan was there, of course, wearing something that looked woven from old Peruvian fishing nets. Other gin-drenched members of the basket-weaving evening class were there too, plus Peter and Geraldine Edgington. Got cornered by verbal bulldozer Daphne Hanson-Hart, who banged on about the war crime of introducing wheelie bins until I lost the will to live.

Later: Hippopotamus ambush, middle of night. No survivors.

Monday 6th February: Frantic for Qinetiq

Last minute flap to get off an application for Qinetiq shares before today's deadline. As an ex-MoD man, this company is right up my street, so I'm glad there was a change of heart about letting in the small investor. With a forward P/E of 11 it isn't even expensive. Brilliant British boffins. Can't beat 'em. Still, hope they haven't offered jobs to many of the MoD managers I had to work with. Take the Bowman infantry radio. While anyone can walk into Phones4U today with £40 and get a mobile that weighs less than a satsuma, we spent more than a decade and £2.5bn on a radio that ended up weighing more than a truck battery (and more than its stone age predecessor, the Clansman), gave its users burns and on which you couldn't even get through to the local Pizza Hut.

Elevenses: Evidence of escaped chimpanzees ransacking the Hornby drawer. Six bananas have appeared. Meanwhile, the remnants of Mr Kipling's almond slice have gone AWOL. Finally, I tackled Eunice.

"Well, Bernard. I have documentary evidence you do eat bananas. I've given up on pears and kiwis."

The armoured slice, as she called it, is in the bin. Took a stealthy look later on, but it's irretrievable, covered with Hermès' leftover cod fillet with parsley sauce. Fussy bloody cat!

Close of play: M&S edged over 500p. Bit worried about this.

Wednesday 8th February: Hells Bells

Inaugural share club meeting in the backroom at the Ring o'Bells in Shensall village. Not been there for years, but it's still got sticky carpets, rickety chairs and overflowing ashtrays. First face I recognise, apart from Mike Delaney's, is the florid mug of Harry Staines, towering at the bar. A well-known ex-Navy man with a line in filthy jokes, Harry is otherwise known as the Rear Admiral after an incident in an Alexandrian brothel in 1962. After getting a round in, Harry introduced Martin Gale, a retired civil engineer and leading light of the local ramblers, and K.P. Sharma, who by reputation made a packet when he sold his chain of convenience stores to Costcutter in 2002. K.P. (Harry immediately asks if it stands for King Prawn) is the only one who is prepared, with carrier bags full of papers and a copy of Company Refs.

After two pints, and some pork pie at the bar, Mike tries to get the meeting underway, but he's no match for Harry, who is in the middle of a joke ("Then the Scotsman said: If that's the best you can do, I'll sleep with the rabbi.") After two more pints, nothing was decided except the club name (Hells Bells. It beat the Clangers by a short head) and nothing remembered by me bar the final line of Harry's joke as I lurched to the gents. "Then Princess Margaret turns around and says to the sepoy: Not in my handbag, you don't."

I'm still trying to work out how it started.

Close of play: Violently ill in the downstairs loo.

Tuesday 14th February: Performance anxiety

Went up to town for Compass AGM at Queen Elizabeth Centre. Dismal, utterly dismal. Not called to give my question, but plenty of others put the boot in. Spent my time among the refreshments looking for Turkey Twizzlers to hurl at the board. Bought Compass shares at 345p in 2004, now 220p. It's tempting to sell, but then if I hadn't owned them I'd be thinking of them as a recovery story. Cash flow is there, dividend yield is 4.6%.

Failed to glean any optimism, especially given what's on the menu later. Eunice has booked a table at Piccolo's, a place the Edgingtons recommended. She says it is intimate (i.e. cramped), ultra chic (over-priced) and romantic (too dim to see the food). Then we have a four-poster room at five-star Downley Grange. "Lovely," I said over breakfast. "How thoughtful of you." Brace yourself Bernard, Valentine's day hippopotamus manoeuvres approach!

Elevenses: Various dodgy-looking Compass comestibles. On the way back bought Eunice a box of Belgian chocolates ("What size would you like sir: The 'overlooked-errand', the 'forgotten anniversary', or the top of the range 'apology for infidelity'?") To go with it picked up one of those sloppy cards with a weary joke about middle age on it. Why is it you can never find the price on them? Price code JJ was all it said. If I'd known it was £2.35p, I'd have made my own card and written a better joke.

Close of Play: M&S closed at 519p. Eek! That's £370 down. Not sure what to do.

Wednesday 15ᵗʰ February: Morning after the fright before

Why do we always choose the grandest surroundings to have a row? We could have had a comfortable cheap falling-out at home, then a British Standard huff and flounce from Eunice. She watches TV, I go to the model railway and separate bedrooms afterwards. Easy as pie. But no, we had a £160 meal at which Eunice quaffed five big glasses of Chablis and flirted with the waiter, then I drove to Downley Grange (£280 a night, excluding breakfast) where I virtually had to carry her, 13 stone of chiffon-clad giggles, up two flights of stairs (hotel too posh for lifts). Then she disappeared into the bathroom long enough for her passport to expire. Bored witless (hotel too posh for TV) , I fished out the latest Railway Modeller. As I heard the lock, I put a pillow over the mag and undid my tie, braced for whatever carnal blitzkrieg was about to be unleashed.

Eunice wobbled towards me, naked except for stiletto heels a bright pink thong, and an odd expression. Sliding her freezing cold hands under my shirt, she whispered that the thong was 'edible.' I replied: "Should have warned me before I ordered that zabaglione, can't eat another morsel."

She hit me with the pillow, thus discovering the Railway Modeller. "How could you, tonight of all nights?" she spat.

"What's the matter, it's not a copy of Mayfair is it?" I retorted.

"No, if only. Then at least I'd know there was some life down there."

So, inexorably, and punctuated by several Oh for God's sake's and You never look at me's we spiralled down into four-poster misery, with not a word exchanged over breakfast or in the car on the way back. Five hundred quid's worth of bust-up.

Elevenses: A banana. One down, five to go.

Close of Play: Spirent falling again, now below 50p. Qinetiq, for some reason I can't fathom is drifting down too, nearly at 200p. Thank God for Bovis, over £8 and going strong.

Tuesday 21ˢᵗ February: Power surge

11pm. Was just watching the Winter Olympics highlights. First time I'd seen curling, apparently derived from northern housework habits. Involves throwing a Russell Hobbs kettle up the ice at two oafs with brooms who have to finish scrubbing the floor before it reaches them. Still, beats sliding down an icy shute on a tea tray, a suicidal pastime which is apparently two events of different names, (skeleton or luge) depending on whether you risk your brains or your balls. Anyway, phone rang.

Mother: "Bernard. The electricity's gone off, they've taken the meter away and I can't find where to put me shillings."

"What are you talking about? You're on direct debit. You don't have a coin meter."

"Well, I must. I put four bob in yesterday. But now I can't find it."

"Are you telling me it's dark? Have you tried all the lights?"

This deranged Mastermind went on for some time (Mrs Dot Jones, you passed on only 19 questions) until I gave up and drove over. It was the fuse of course, but Dot had indeed been feeding coins (5p pieces, £2 coins, and the odd pfennig) into the gap under the gas meter, and I needed a screwdriver to get them out. Frustrating, yes, but nothing compared to the fate that befell me on Wednesday.

Chapter Seven

An Arresting Experience

Wednesday 22nd February: Driven to distraction

Terrifying day! Jem had been badgering me to go and help her remove her belongings from the flat she shared with gay Toby and bring them here so she can rent it out. So I hired a van, left it outside here last night hoping for an early start today. But at 7am have a discovery: Someone has bashed into it, scraped the side, and left the driver-side wing mirror dangling. Great! That's £200 in excess up the Swanny.

Already fuming, arrive in Fulham to discover Jem's "few bits and bobs" would fill an airship hangar. She's no help on furniture-lifting either ("Daddy, I've broken a nail!"), so it was muggins here with high cholesterol and low back pain who did the work. Didn't finish until 5pm, and traffic out of Fulham was awful. Two hours later, halfway between Sevenoaks and Tonbridge, traffic on the A21 comes to a standstill. Police helicopters overhead, sirens ahead. Kept thinking: Must be one heck of a pile up. Must get the van unloaded and back by 10pm to avoid another day's charge, so see a side road on the left 200 yards further up, and slip out onto the verge to scoot along to it. All this is hard enough, as Jem has so much stuff on her lap in the cab (including a 4' suede-covered pig called Prescott) I can't even see the remaining mirror, but soon we are whizzing up a country lane. Then some noisy bloody motorcycle is on my tail, can't see him but he won't overtake, so I put my foot down. Helicopter noises get louder, and suddenly there are sirens ahead, and round a corner two police cars parked across the road.

"Daddy, stop! They've got guns!" Jem screams, but it's too late and I turn sharp left and plough into a hedge instead. Hit my head on the wheel, and Jem, who'd used the seat belt to secure her box of bloody teddy bears instead of herself, ends up across the dashboard.

"Armed police!," is the next I hear but I'm already cradling a whimpering Jemima in my arms and looking at a smear of blood on the windscreen when the door is ripped open by some burly copper who points a sub-machine gun in my face and bellows: "Come on Fossett, you're nicked!"

Who the hell is Fossett?

Close of play: Banged up at Paddington Green while two coppers keep asking me where I've stashed the cash, and "Who's the mole at Securitas". They won't listen to my protestations, and ignore my pleas about Jem. Instead they wave the van paperwork in front of me bellowing: "Come on Fossett, couldn't you think of a better alias than Jones!"

It's almost midnight when a female inspector comes in and admits that they've got the wrong man. Jem, apparently is OK, just bruises. No apologies, no contrition, just a final kick up the backside. I'm to be charged with driving without due care and attention! Still, the interrogation I got from Eunice as she drove me home made the Met look like beginners.

2.30am: Got home. Hugged Jemima, poor bruised thing, for the longest time since she was a child. Tears all round.

Thursday 8ᵗʰ March: The wheelie thing

4.45am. Dreaming of African exploration, my bearers struggling in the heat with their load of cherry bakewells and eccles cakes as we wade across crocodile infested rivers (and particularly alert for hippopotamus manoeuvres). Then the sound of tom-toms, coming closer and closer. Struggle awake. Peek between the curtains, fully expecting to see massed hordes of Watusi warriors pillaging Endsleigh Gardens.

The reality is more horrifying. Workmen are hurling wheelie bins off the back of an enormous lorry onto the street, where they crash and boom. Goblin-like figures swarm around them, dragging them into inconvenient places where they block drives, hem in parked vehicles and occupy pavements. Suddenly a light goes on at number 43, and a door bursts open showering the scene with the light of righteousness. There in the doorway, clad only in a quilted pink housecoat and fluffy slippers, and armed only with a broom is Daphne Hanson-Hart, paladin royal and scourge of the council Waste Services Team. A halogen halo lights her recently-permed crown as she gallops down her path toward the massed enemy beyond. A large bespectacled hobgoblin, clad in high-visibility tunic over a shirt and tie draws his clipboard and prepares to block her path. Though he is fully a foot taller than her, fear is a stranger to this warrior queen. Proudly she chants words of power, the wagging finger smiting her way into the heart of the enemy. Taken aback by the ferocity of her attack, Waste Services regroups by the back of their lorry, gesticulating in turn and holding up their magical clipboard of 'orders from a higher authority'. Undeterred, Daphne smites a green wheelie bin with the shaft of her broom, toppling it into the gutter. In desperation, one Waste Services operative clambers back into the lorry, which

66

roars into life. Orange lights flash and a piercing Beep-Beep-Beep is emitted by the monster as it reverses towards her, breathing deadly diesel. Undaunted, she stands her ground, striking the steel dragon with her broom. Now, from further up the road comes the cavalry. Mr and Mrs Oliver Pendlewood, in matching lavender bathrobes are pushing back their wheelie bins towards the lorry. Mrs Davidson, waving a letter, is taken on by the chief hobgoblin with his clipboard.

After a frantic mêlée of pointing and gesticulating, Waste Services is overmastered. They load back half a dozen bins, and drive away leaving the spoils of victory to the residents of Endsleigh Gardens.

Saturday 11th March: Key of life

Glory be, I've found the key! It was in the case of an old pair of reading glasses (one of nine lost around the house in 18 months) The Hornby drawer is now secure. No more kiwi fruit, no inscrutable Chinese pears, just good solid British bickies. Notice that Nasdaq has made a bid approach to the London Stock Exchange. Time to open a museum for bowler hats and black brollies?

Monday 13th March: Marks Expensive

Misery. Post brings bill for £200 excess on the van, notice of prosecution and reminder for first instalment on the damn conservatory. Builders aren't due to start work until next month! Perhaps we should have gone with Ultraframe, they certainly need the work and it would have been cheaper. Final nail in the coffin, some spiv from the spread-betting company phones up and demands £464! Tells me that M&S have shot up to 562p, eaten up all my margin, and if I want to keep my short position I shall have to "pony up and pronto", otherwise I'll have to cut my losses. Have to admit I hadn't kept my eye on this ball for weeks, and this sends me into a panic.

"What should I do?" I ask him, and he says smugly, "Sorry Sir, we're not allowed to give investment advice." Can't bear to let Stuart Rose get one over on me, so I say I'll pay up. Damn!

Elevenses: Two delicious fresh cream éclairs (buy one get one free, how could I resist?) from the bakers, the box concealed under my coat to get past Eunice security and into the den! Somehow this makes me feel like a cholesterol suicide bomber.

Saturday 18th March: Chinese paper torture

Breakfast guerrilla games again. Eunice waits until I have my head well into the paper and then starts wittering at me. Today, the only day of the week I take the FT, I was well into a brain-stretching analysis by Martin Wolf. I'd just reached a paragraph which started 'Seventhly, Chinese GDP growth...' and then she launched in.

"Don't forget you've got to see your mother next week."

I grunted my assent. Then there was a short pause before: "You'll need to fill the Volvo up before you go, it's on the red."

Yes I know. Then there is a thirty second pause and it will be something else. Concentration finally interrupted I lower the paper to find she has finished wittering, and is herself reading a magazine, curling a finger through her hair as if nothing had happened. Only when the paper goes back up ('And eighthly, the motive for holding U.S. Treasury bonds...') Then she launches in again. This little charade can go on for hours. I recall nothing I was reading, yet no information of any value is passed across by Eunice either. No, the point of the exercise is to get attention. To compete with and (yes!) defeat the hated newspaper.

Sunday 19th March: Fears and prostration

Lengthy breakfast skirmish, machine gunned with trivia while I try to read about Vodafone's boardroom quarrels. Finally I drop the Telegraph and ask her to tell me whatever it is she wants to say. First she accuses me of being testy for rattling the paper, then she says:

"Bernard, have you ever had your prostate checked?"

No, I reply.

"Well you do have problems with your urinary tract, don't you?"

Urinary tract? Why doesn't she just say waterworks? I'm sure she's been reading American medical journals on the Internet again.

"You are up twice or three times every night," she continues. I respond that it's just a bit of a dickey bladder, no trouble at all.

"Well you keep getting up wakes *me* up, and then I lie awake worrying that you might have problems."

Problems? Nothing a little wife strangling couldn't sort. However I tell her I feel fine.

"Ah but there are often no symptoms."

"No symptoms of *what*, for God's sake?"

"Prostate cancer."

"I don't have cancer, Eunice. Stop fretting."

"Bernard. One man in six gets it. Do think about it, it's Prostate Awareness Week next week."

The week after, I respond, is Holiday from Harridans Week. Exit one bristling Eunice. Slammed door.

Tuesday 21st March: Prostate Awareness Week

Eunice somehow has laid hands on a 'prostate awareness' badge, and has pinned it to her cardigan. She hasn't said any more, but clearly I'm going to get no peace on the issue. I sigh deeply, ring the quack and make an appointment. Dr Ross, 3.45pm on Friday. Never heard of him. Why can't I ever get to see my own doctor?

Elevenses: Plain chocolate Bounty. Being good, only eat half.

Close of Play: M&S continues to climb. Now 573p. Help!

Wednesday 22nd March: Budget day

Biggest hot air-to-action ratio ever. Munched entire multi-pack of Hula Hoops while watching Brown drone. Feel queasy now. Salt-overdose? Nerves about Friday's appointment?

Friday 24th March: The NHS digital advance

Just got back from quack's, in a state of shock. First off, walked in to the consulting room and found Dr Ross was not male at all. In fact a loud, industrial-size version of Ann Widdecombe. Asked me horrendous waterworks questions, culminating in: "How often do you have sex?" I exaggerated and said once a month. Then without looking up from her form, she said "How about masturbation?"

"Not at the moment, thanks all the same."

"Mr Jones." She glared at me over her glasses. "How often? Once a day, once a week?"

So began the lecture. Apparently the old prostate needs flushing out, and regularly bashing the bishop, particularly in your twenties and thirties, keeps it in fine fettle. I wish they'd let me know when I was fifteen. I'd kept it down to thrice daily out of fear of blindness.

The quack sat me on the bed took a blood sample, and then said to be on the safe side she would do a digital check of the prostate, and would I be kind enough to slip off my clothes.

"Oh," I said. "I thought being the NHS the machines would still be analogue." For some reason she found this hilarious, but I

70

was so relieved there wasn't going to be the rumoured prodding I'd heard about that I didn't give it a second thought. Then I heard the stretch and snap of latex gloves, looked over my shoulder as the curtains parted and saw the digit she had in mind.

"Come on Mr Jones. Bend over. And do try to relax."

Chapter Eight

Anno Domini

Wednesday 29th March: No such thing as a free lunch

Share club meeting. Serious drinking probable, so got Eunice to give me a lift. Mistake. Only she can overtake at 60mph in 2nd gear, then ask what "that funny screaming noise" is. Only she can make me flinch at every bend or junction, make me stamp on imaginary brakes and stare in horror at the road ahead.

Immediate double scotch on arrival at the Ring o'Bells to quell quivering. Harry Staines already on his second pint and third punch line. ("'Oh', she says. 'If I knew you'd got ten pounds I'd have taken me tights off.'")

Mike Delaney calls the meeting to order. Decided to set a variable contribution level, with units to match. Like Mike Delaney I'm going for £50 a month (could have been £100 but for that M&S margin call). Harry reckons he can only manage £20 but K.P. is going for the maximum £200. Got ribbed (again) over my van chase and arrest.

Elevenses: Bowl of free crisps at the bar. Tasted appalling, so I asked the barmaid what flavour they were. The girl, a pale spiky-haired creature with numerous rings in her eyebrows (does she wear curtains at night?) poked through the bin until she found the packet. "Says here 'Roasted Mediterranean vegetable, organic sun-dried tomato an' drizzled with extra virgin olive oil flavour'," adding "best before July 2003."

Seeing my expression she added "Well, that's why it's free ain't it? I can get yer a bag of salt n' vinegar for 40p."

"Done."

Thursday 30th March: Queen's Gambit

M&S, thankfully, are slipping a little. Still, my short spread-bet is nearly £1,000 in the red, given that I set it at 482p and the shares have climbed to 570p. I've got a couple of successes, though. BAe, bought in October 2005 for 330p is now at 420p, and Bovis is going great guns. Bought at 660p in December, now just below 950p! Portfolio added £2,014 so far this year.

Quack's receptionist phoned and whinged that I haven't followed up my cholesterol test with an appointment to talk about diet. I reluctantly agree to do so, then get put through to the dreaded Dr Ross who has my prostate test results, conveniently rendered into Sanskrit. "The protein specific antigen test confirmed my initial hypothesis of benign prostatic hypertrophy." Reckon I should get a bloody trophy, considering what she put me through.

Elevenses: Now lockable, Hornby drawer contains an Aladdin's cave of secrets: An entire packet of all-butter Scottish shortbread, a Mr Kipling treacle tart, two Crunchies and, cunningly, an apple. This I can whip out if the tyrant queen demands to know what is concealed within.

Friday 31st March: Birthday neglect

I'm 63 tomorrow. In mirror, face is a battlefield of disappointments, fringed in fading grey. Live a kind of cowering existence, flitting from model railway in the loft to computer in the den, dreams confined to Great Western Region rolling stock or stock market riches. Reality? Last week Eunice went through my wardrobe to make space for Jemima's wagon train of clothes and shoes. I found my old brogues, still gleaming from 20 years of daily polishing, in a box destined for Age Concern, together with Eunice's old lampshades, and an Emmerdale video. Was I asked? Not at all.

Elevenses: Three shortbread bickies.
Close of Play: Down £203.76

Saturday 1ˢᵗ April: Wrong kind of birthday coach

Presents: Signal box from Brian and Janet. Bag of lichen and bark allegedly from the Antichrist, but clearly bought and labelled by Janet. Bottle of Glenfiddich from Jemima, v. nice. Eunice must have misread my list. Instead of the pair of GWR 1930s coaches I requested, she has bought me a 12-part life coaching course. I gazed at the book and DVD with speechless amazement. It was entitled 'Hug the inner you'. On the cover was a tanned 8' tall lantern-jawed American with a halogen smile, and his arms around some 25-year old swimsuited Barbie doll. 'Our promise: To unzip the bold, confident you.' It went on: 'renew the body, rebuild the mind, to hug that heart within.'

Eunice said: "Come on Bernard. You just seem so down recently. I've been at a bit of a loss, what with you avoiding me and glaring at everyone. So I was talking about it to Irmgard, and she recommended this to build your self-confidence."

At that point I went ballistic: "Don't discuss our life with that nosy hag! In two seconds she'll have us all in a Welsh peasant collective, colonically irrigated and munching organic kelp. This Californian new age tosh is appalling. How much did you pay for it?" Eunice hesitated, before whispering "Um, £112 I think."

"What!" I roared.

Then she added sheepishly: "Plus VAT. Per month. I'm afraid I signed up for the first six months in advance. I thought you'd approve, we get a 10% discount."

Aarrgh!

Sunday 2ⁿᵈ April : Dinner at the Edgingtons

All morning up in the loft, putting together the signal box and seeing where on the layout it will go best. Have refused to look at the 'Heart hugging' book or DVD. What utter tosh!

Elevenses: Small sliver of treacle tart, while I read the Compass annual report. Dismal stuff. I really should sell, but what of the losses?

Later: Dinner at Peter and Geraldine Edgington's. Endured alleged Ardennes pate which tasted like a briquette of Kit-e-Kat. While Geraldine held Eunice spellbound with details of her cellulite removal cream, Peter guided me away up to his office. He claims to keeps a simple portfolio and never trade, except regular as clockwork to sell in May before they go off to their villa in Capri. Reckons to beat the FTSE 100 every year by at least a point or two.

"Did you find out about that company history?" he asked. I tell him the entire Marconi tragedy, how it was a certificate in English Electric left to my mother. I do not, though, let on to the scale of the loss, and feign a c'est la vie attitude.

"Sympathies, old man," he says. "I know you've had a few rough patches, what with Compass, Spirent et al. Perhaps it would make sense to go the funds route?" I takes me a while to realise what an insult this is. Fuming.

Monday 3ʳᵈ April: Builder's bum

Hammering on the door at 11.15am, shortly after Eunice had set off for Waitrose. Open it to see three spotty oiks in overalls and beyond a giant van parked athwart the pavement.

"Winduz?" says one. I beg his pardon.

"New winduz, rahnd the back, yeah?".

"Ah, you've come to build the new conservatory?"

"Yeah, s'mostly winduz innit?"

"I was hoping for a roof and some foundations, if it's not too much trouble," I respond, adding that I was expecting them at 8am.

"Facking M25 innit," was the concise explanation. After copious cups of sugary tea, they start work and as I retreat to the loft I hear the ululation of Radio Liquid Brain 78.2FM punctuated by hammering noises and the f-word without which no communication, however basic, can be conveyed.

Elevenses: Crunchie bar, munched noisily to drown out the din.

By 2pm all has gone quiet. Hear Eunice arrive, the rustle of upper class supermarket bags and then: "BERNARD!!!" With a sinking feeling, I scramble down to the dining room where Eunice's finger is quivering towards a large gap in the wall, where our french windows used to be, and through a sheet of plastic, a heap of bricks and rubble on the flower beds beyond. No sign of the oiks, but dirty footprints, crisp packets and scattered mugs indicate some activity. The room, open to the elements, is absolutely freezing.

I know with the certainty of experience, that despite this being *her* idea, *her* conservatory, *her* £50,000 extravaganza, this ultimately will all be *my* fault.

Tuesday 4th April: Team coach

8am. No sign of builders. Firm's HQ is on answering machine. Incandescent! Just about to try again when phone rings. It's an American voice, and irritatingly cheerful.

"Hi, is this B'nard Jones?"

"No, I'm BERnud Jones. And who pray are you?"

"Praying's not part of the course, Bernie. I'm Josh Fenderbrun, your life coach."

"No you're not. You're a damn nuisance. I have no need of a life coach. Please send my wife's money back, forthwith. Good day." Slam phone down. Thirty seconds later he phones back, all breezy chat, insisting my previous conversation just proved how essential life coaching was to me.

"Your wife knows you better than anyone, B'nard. She's investing in your future. Trust to her instincts and let me teach you to hug your heart."

At this point I use the builders' favourite word, together with several of my own. This time *he* hangs up.

Elevenses: Five shortbread biscuits and two paracetamol.

Close of play: Up a couple of hundred, which is encouraging, except Qinetiq is falling again. God, it's freezing in here. Tried securing the builders' plastic sheet when the rain started tipping down, but the carpet and coffee table got damp, including water company's notification of drought order.

Evening: Peter Edgington phoned at 10.15pm, v. late for him. Seems he's been ruminating over the Marconi fiasco.

"Bernard, you know this e-mail from Telent. Did it mention anything about British Aerospace?" I respond that yes, I vaguely recall a mention.

"It's just that BAe bought a chunk of GEC in 1999. From memory I think they paid in shares. Perhaps you should check it?"

I mumble my thanks, though I'm still a bit doubtful. Seems irrelevant though. If Marconi went up the Swanny then it hardly matters what they were given, does it? Eunice, a vision in puce housecoat and fluffy slippers, thrusts a mug of BournVita into my hand.

"Bernard, leave it to the morning, for goodness sake and come to bed."

Wednesday 5th April: Down to business at Hell's Bells

No clean underwear, so forced to wear those awful M&S tartan boxers. Phoned builders at 8am. Blew up at manager, who said they would send someone over to review the work so far. Review what? They haven't bloody done anything except make a giant hole in the back of the house. Windows and skip to be delivered today, apparently. At least it's warmer now. Life coach Josh Fenderbrun phoned again, and was particularly difficult to get rid of. Asked about my ambitions, to which I offered: "To be left alone by nosy Yanks". He seems v. hard to offend.

Elevenses: Packet of pork scratching followed by a ploughman's. Ring o'Bells share club meeting finally gets down to business i.e. what are we going to buy. Mike Delaney notes the FTSE has climbed five per cent since our first meeting in February while we dithered. K.P. Sharma has an explanation: "You all drink too much. We can't make decisions like that. We have to be analytical, but alcohol makes you emotional."

Harry Staines, florid-faced as ever says "Well, I'll drink to that!" drains his pint, and orders another. Mike suggests we all each make a pitch for a share to buy this week. So, in turn we do. Harry, after a two decades as a car dealer reckons we should go for luxury car distributor European Motors Holdings, I suggest newly cheap Qinetiq, while Martin Gale is all for going for some tiny oil explorer called Fortune Oil. K.P Sharma is the most convincing though, he's a big fan of BHP Billiton because of its exposure to all the commodities including oil. Explains the super cycle theory which reckons we've got a couple of decades at least of higher prices for copper, zinc etc. Though BHP's gone up a lot, at £11 or so the forward P/E is just over 10, which he reckons is cheap. In the end we mandate K.P. to make the purchase. Sadly, we'll only be able to afford 100 shares. Still, it's a start.

Close of play: Return to find a skip on the drive blocking the entrance to the garage. Impotent rage (The purest kind).

Thursday 6th April: A-day

Between bombarding the builders with calls about the skip, peruse acres of newsprint about the A-day pension reform. Doesn't affect me, thanks to the MoD pension, but I know perfect Peter Edgington had high hopes for getting a buy-to-let in his SIPP. Can't restrain my feelings of schadenfreude now that he can't. Perhaps I'm just an embittered and envious old goat.

Elevenses: An eccles cake, which once again exploded over my keyboard. Took me 15 minutes to get the crumbs out. Must remember to re-read that enormous e-mail from Telent to see if what Peter said makes sense. Still doubt there's any money in it. Don't get the chance because Eunice, claiming she has a painful bunion wants me to drive her to the chiropodist. She hobbles like a war hero into the Volvo, biting her lip. On arrival, notice the chiropodist is now a podiatrist, just like opticians have mutated into optometrists. As I once said to the osteopath who complained that I called him a chiropractor, it makes bugger all difference except we have to pay more. He gave my head an extra sharp twist for that.

Post-treatment, Eunice then finagled me into taking her on some extensive shoe shopping ("Bernard, I really don't have any comfortable shoes"). She was across the threshold of Clark's like a bloody greyhound.

Later: While we're watching TV, Eunice complained about my alleged 'harrumphing.'

"What do you mean," I asked. "I don't 'harrumph'."

"Bernard, you've *always* harrumphed. Ever since Harold Wilson got back in. But you do it more and more. At the BBC news, Newsnight, the Today programme, in fact anything on Radio 4. But it's really got out of hand now. Good God, Bernard, we're watching Emmerdale! What on earth is there to disapprove of in Emmerdale?

Friday 7ᵗʰ April : Fabulous discovery

Following Peter Edgington's advice, finally got round to re-reading the Telent e-mail. Yes indeed British Aerospace did offer shares in itself in exchange for acquiring Marconi Electronic Systems for £7.7bn. After reading the whole thing through twice, the penny finally dropped. BAe wasn't giving shares to GEC/Marconi the company but to the *shareholders* in GEC/Marconi. Each shareholder got about a half a share in BAE for each GEC share they held, on a separate certificate. Plus some loan stock which has since been repaid. So Dad's 100,000 English Electric shares, which became 333,332 in GEC, then each inherited 0.428792819 shares in BAe which, my lying Woolworth's calculator assures me is 142,930 shares in BAe! Multiplied by £4.20 that is £600,000. I can't believe it! Those 100,000 English Electric shares have finally come good, and dotty Dot is going to get her money.

Chapter Nine

Unwelcome Interruptions

Saturday 8th April: In the forests of the night

Dot phoned at 2am, in some anxiety. Tigers are apparently growling under her bedroom window.

"Mum," I respond. "There are no tigers in Isleworth. Not any more. I believe they went extinct in the 1970s. Domestic cats perhaps?"

I hear the sound of her opening the window. "No, look. One's got stripes," she says in finality. "Oh, and a bell round its neck."

"Not likely to be a tiger, Mum. It's a size thing really. If they bother you, throw a bucket of water over them."

"Hot or cold?" she asks. Cold, I explain, will do fine. Mollified, she hangs up and I can get back to sleep. Except I lie awake, wondering at what stage to try to explain to my dotty 89-year-old mother about her vast increase in wealth. Eunice, meanwhile, snored through it all. Perhaps I should phone Dot back: "That," I would say holding the receiver over Eunice's open mouth, "That's what a tiger sounds like." Eventually I fall asleep, dream of gaining power of attorney. Wake up drenched with guilt.

Tuesday 11th April: Mr Annoying calls

Awful day. 7.45am. Doorbell, persistently rung. Pad down in bathrobe, hear cheery whistling as I open front door. See besuited Alan Titchmarsh look-alike, rows of biros in breast pocket.

"Morning, Raymond's the name. I've come to inspect the conservatory."

"I presume you can see invisible objects?" I retort.

He pads through, gets out his clipboard. Starts sucking his teeth, tutting, jotting notes. He even says "Oh dear, oh dear, oh dear." Finally, he turns to me. "They've not even started the foundations you know," he says.

"Yes, I know. I've been trying to tell you for a week!"

"That's all wrong."

"Yes, I know."

"The Dartford foundations team should have been here last week, but the Colchester office seems to have sent the windows boys. Now, I've been in this business a long time. And you can't start with the windows, you know. It's got to be foundations, every time. Then floor, then walls."

"Oh, really, can't you start with the roof?" I growl.

"Sarcasm, sarcasm," he tuts, getting back to his jotting. He looks through the side window.

"Ooh, look where they left the skip. They shouldn't have left it there. I expect that's blocking in your garage. Still, that's Colchester for you."

I'm just about to strangle this brylcreemed gnome, when Jemima hisses down the stairs "Daddy, someone on the phone, says it's urgent."

It's the bloody spread-bet company. They want another £562 right away or they're going to close the M&S short position.

The shares have just leapt to 593p from 561p yesterday and my equity was apparently already too low anyway.

I concede defeat. From 482p on Friday 13th January, M&S has soared 113p, and at £10 a point I've lost £1,200 or so including the interest. Dot may have £600,000 worth of BAe shares, but right now I'm short of cash.

Elevenses: Lock myself in the loft with two slices of battenburg for consolation. Ate the yellow cake squares first and re-wrapped the marzipan around the red cake squares before nibbling off the corners. Childhood, I decide, is wasted on the young.

Wednesday 19th April: Mooning for profit

Share club meeting. K.P Sharma starts explaining his company refs with all its moons, half full, empty or whatnot, as a way to spot what you want in the investing firmament. Harry Staines is dubious. He says his own experience of mooning, involving a minor member of the Royal Family, would have got him a dishonourable discharge in 1961 except the lady in question was too short-sighted to see from the Portsmouth quay to the deck of HMS Repulsive. " Moving swiftly on," as K.P. is wont to say, we discuss commodities again.

Just as K.P. is talking about copper prices rising again, the dark spiky-haired barmaid (she of the eyebrow rings) says: "Nah, you'll get clouted if you do that."

Open-mouthed, we look up as she clears the glasses.

"Copper's riding for a fall in the next month or two," she says. "I know 'cos Dad's in the recycling business. You wouldn't believe how much copper scrap is worth now. He's buying lorry-loads of old computers and stuff, plumbers leftovers, you name it."

"Why computers?" asks K.P.

"A PC is about 10 per cent copper by weight," she says . Lots of it is tied in to circuit boards, and isn't easy to get at, but the new EU recycling directive regulation, really aimed at batteries, will mean lots of PCs and laptops will now have to be taken apart. There's huge amounts of metal in a PC power supply and back-up batteries, and Dad is getting in now while it's cheap."

Chantelle, as we discover, is a bright young thing. In the end she asks if she can join the club. She can only contribute £20 a month, but that's fine by us.

Friday 21ˢᵗ April: Cyst assistant

Disturbed breakfast. Happily sitting eating a boiled egg and reading the Telegraph when Eunice, who'd been on the phone for more than half an hour thundered downstairs and announced breathlessly: "Janet's got an ovarian cyst."

I examined Eunice's face for clues as to how I should react. Clearly there was a cause of some excitement. I took a wild stab: "Is that one of those Irish designer handbags?"

"Bernard, the doctor's sending her straight to hospital. It's endometrial and they're going to perform a laparotomy."

"Didn't Daley Thompson do one of those after he won gold?"

After being berated for a few minutes for my lack of knowledge or interest in women's bits, Eunice laid out a plan of campaign with a practised ease which would not have disgraced Rommel. Our daughter-in-law would be heading off to hospital this morning, with no time to do the supermarket run. We'd need to shop for them, pick up Digby from school and baby-sit until Brian got home. He'd then head off to see Janet in hospital, Eunice would go with him (presumably to lecture the consultants on exactly what they should do), while I would entertain the mephistophelian munchkin until his bedtime, which was 8pm.

Elevenses. With the household's mental air raid sirens ringing, I was not allowed to retreat into the den. Instead, forced to partake of half a pear with Eunice while she reeled off gynaecological horror stories that had happened to her friends over the years, culminating in the tale, dredged up from the early 1980s, of Daphne Hanson-Hart's ectopic pregnancy. Eunice interprets my lack of interest as ignorance.

"Bernard, it shocks me that you have no idea what an ectopic pregnancy is."

"I have never heard of an ectope, so how they breed is of no interest. If I wanted to know I'd tune into Living Planet."

"You're just trying to twist things. You've misquoted me again, word for word."

3pm: Headed off to Sainsbury's. Eunice is reviewing Janet's shopping list, which is almost the size of Whitaker's Almanack. We, apparently, are going to need three trolleys. The supermarket turns out to be the size of the Cardington airship hangar, and has an entire aisle labelled 'deodorants'. A little put off by the size of the place, Eunice circles the trolleys by the lager section and stands guard while I'm dispatched with a hand basket for some long range reconnaissance. My task, should I choose to accept it, is to hunt down mysterious and rarely-seen items, to wit: cinnamon grahams, pimento-stuffed Tuscan olives, the 18kg industrial-size drum of salad cream in the 'Basics' range (the only approved fuel for the family's satanic offspring), and some half-fat organic Welsh goat yoghurt.

"Is there a brand for that?" I ask Eunice.

"Yes. Janet wasn't sure of the name, but it begins with an L'

"An L? That's a handy clue for a Welsh name."

"Some Ls anyway. And there's a Y in it somewhere."

As I trudge off, Eunice squawks after me: "…And don't get any other brand. Brian won't eat Muller Lite. And Digby comes up in boils when he eats those little Danone things."

Fifteen minutes later, I'm lost. I'm at the intersection of 'patio heaters' avenue and 'feminine hygiene products' boulevard and I can no longer see anything edible. There are no staff around, and the only other customer nearby is a dumpy cross-eyed woman, whose trolley is a clinking emplacement of Carling, sandbagged with jumbo packets of Hula Hoops. Hanging from this all-terrain vehicle, three shrieking children are fighting for possession of an Armalite-sized plastic water gun, presumably stocked in 'irritating and antisocial toys' drive.

"Excuse, me can you direct me towards…food?" I ask her.

"Oh, yes. Food. I did see some, up on the left. Past school uniforms and slippers. There's bound to be something to eat down there. Will you be alright until then, or would you like some Hula Hoops?" she asks, waving a packet the same size as a pillow.

"No it's fine. I left my wife there."

Half an hour and 32 aisles away, I find Eunice in a state of agitation. Her wagon train of groceries has come to a halt in the foothills of the Andes of Andrex.

"Bernard, where have you been! We were supposed to pick Digby up from school at four, and its already quarter past."

"He'll have walked home, won't he? It isn't far."

"Yes, but he won't be able to get in."

As we hurry out, Eunice fills me in on the campaign so far. The yoghurt has sold out, and the cinnamon grahams are no longer on special offer, so she only bought six packets. The salad cream has been located, and the stuffed olives liberated. I'm absolutely exhausted, and still have an evening's babysitting of the tyrant tyke to go.

The final straw. Five minutes from Brian and Janet's and we're crawling in heavy traffic along red route territory. Eunice notices a health food shop and insists I stop so she can look for the damned Welsh yoghurt. I ask her to hold on for a moment, until I can park, but no, she flings the door open without looking and suddenly there's a wallop, and a gymnastic cartwheel onto the pavement involving high visibility clothing, cap, torch, radio and other sundry items: Eunice has knocked a Community Support Officer off his mountain bike.

Saturday 22nd April: Mills and Boon

Still stuck at Brian and Janet's with Digby. Amazingly, Eunice escaped with a caution for her savage and unprovoked attack on the constabulary. Perhaps they were swayed by her Florence Nightingale impression, but it didn't fool me. Tearing open the young man's uniform and feeling his hairy chest might have won her a Mills and Boon fantasy medicine award, but seeing as the poor fellow had only been winded and chipped a tooth it was medically unnecessary.

"Are you a nurse?" the poor man had muttered while Eunice laid my Harris tweed jacket in the filthy gutter for him to lay his head upon.

"No, but I've seen every series of Holby City," she cooed, stroking his forehead.

Meanwhile, I've got a £140 bill from the Dent Doctor for removing teeth marks from the Volvo's near side door. Janet is on the mend after her whateveritscalled-oscopy and will be back this afternoon. Brian is still at the hospital, so I've drawn the short straw. I'm tasked with preparing lunch for the fussiest child on the planet, a process requiring more care and planning than removing spent uranium fuel rods from Sellafield. I start with a casual tone.

"What do you normally have for lunch, Digby?"

"Chicken McNuggets at McDonalds."

Nice try, I have to admit. "Now, Digby I know that Janet doesn't approve of McDonalds. How about sharing a couple of slices of Welsh rarebit with your good old grandad?"

"Uurgh….What's that?"

"It's cheese on toast.."

"I don't like cheese. And I hate toast."

"You can't hate toast. No-one hates toast."

"I do. It's rubbish."

"It's just cooked bread."

"I don't like bread."

"Digby, don't lie to me. I've seen you eat bread. What about those salad cream sandwiches."

"Yeah, but I can't taste the bread then."

"Well you won't taste this. Its Sunblest. There's nothing in it and it has no flavour. It's designed to hold things. Like cheese for example."

"I hate cheese."

"Digby there are hundreds of types of cheese, so you can't say you don't like them all."

"But Mum only gets cheddar. I hate cheddar. I don't mind a salad cream sandwich though."

"You can't have a salad cream sandwich."

"Why not?"

"There's no nutritional value in it."

"Grandma says that you hide food which is all sugary in a secret drawer at home. Mum say sugar isn't good for you."

That child is too clever by half. "What I eat for elevenses isn't my lunch, Digby. It's in addition to a nutritious lunch. You're young and you need vitamins to help you grow properly."

"But I'm tall for my age, Grandad."

So in the end we went to McDonalds.

Wednesday 26th April: Money talks

Share club meeting at Ring o'Bells. Mike Delaney had given us his apologies, and everyone had brought along an annual report so that K.P. Sharma, the only one of us who knew anything about accounting, could test our knowledge.

"These are bigger and more boring than my old bat's underwear," said Harry Staines, as he tossed a Vodafone annual review onto the pile among the beer glasses. "I can't get my head around gearing, amortisation and stuff like that."

"The thing is, Harry," K.P. said "That if you don't understand how balance sheets are built, and what can and can't go on them, you don't know what you've actually bought in a share. If you can spot a company that has assets like property which are in reality worth more than the share price values at them, you have an absolute bargain."

"But how can anyone do that with Vodafone. There's an army of share analysts crawled all over it," Harry retorted.

"True," said K.P., but if you apply the same rules to a smaller and less well-researched company, you might do well."

Harry was spending more time looking at Chantelle. Our resident goth was wearing a pink duffel-coat type woollen dress with a tatty black basque over the top and long motorcycle boots. While Harry was clearly interested in this unique and risqué ensemble, and the curves it emphasised, to me she looked more like a mobile Barnardo's outlet.

Martin Gale expressed all our frustration when he suggested that we really needed more money to make fresh investments. "This is what I wanted to join a share club to do. But we've only got a few hundred quid," he said.

"Well, I did suggest that we had a more substantial minimum investment," said K.P. Sharma. "But you all voted me down."

"Well, we don't have the lolly," said Harry. "Bernard's weighed down by his wife's conservatory, Martin's up to his neck in debt, Mike's got a 30-a-day fag habit, and Chantelle's on minimum wage. I'm not doing any better. The Jag's been off the road for three months now, and it'll cost me a grand to get it sorted so I'm ready to use it when my ban expires. That's if I can afford the insurance."

Chantelle looked puzzled. "Harry, how does someone who lives two doors down from the pub ever need to drink-drive?"

"I didn't! It was after Sunday lunch chucking-out time at the Harrow, and I knew I shouldn't drive so I kipped in the car for a while. My mistake was to be parked on double yellows and have the engine on to keep the heater going."

This was an edited version of the story I'd heard before. "Harry, from what I recall the bigger mistake was to offer the young WPC who arrested you 'a good seeing-to' on condition she let you go."

"Well, she had a face like a weasel's divorce, so I thought I do her a favour."

"Do her a favour!" Chantelle grimaced at Harry's bilberry-hued nose, ruddy face and sporadic teeth. "No mirrors in your house then, Harry?"

The aged lothario's self confidence was miraculous. "It's all about personality, my Darling. Age doesn't matter. Look at Bruce Forsyth, look at Hugh Hefner, look at whatsisname, Onassis. Look at John Prescott, for Christ's sake."

"That's money and power, not personality," Chantelle insisted, as the rest of us dissolved into laughter.

Harry, now in his element continued. "No, no. Take Henry Kissinger. Ugly as a warthog's thong. Not proper rich, but pulled a sexy young thing. If even he can, I don't see why Harry Staines couldn't tempt a mangy police dog."

"Sexist!" we all bellowed, but only Chantelle really meant it.

"Alright," said Harry. "You want evidence? In the last five years I've had the landlady of the Harrow…."

"You've had Majorie Bellingham? You dirty dog!" Martin muttered.

"…both the lunchtime barmaids at the Fox and Hounds, busty Beatrice from the cold meat counter at the Co-op, and a West Indian traffic warden called Annie or Anneliese or something."

"Bullshit," we all roared.

"I'll tell your wife," Chantelle teased.

"She wouldn't believe you."

"We don't believe you, either," I said. "I think Chantelle's right. No twenty-five year old woman is going to be attracted to anyone over sixty unless he's loaded."

"In which case," Martin said. "Let's get this bloody share club on the road to riches. I'm twenty years younger than Harry, and I'm clearly not getting my share."

K. P. Sharma had been silent for some minutes. "This is all *disgusting*. Listening to you, I can't believe the British have the nerve to accuse Asian men of not treating women with respect."

"Okay," said Martin. "Fair enough, but when are we going to start getting results with these shares?"

K. P. let out a gasp of exasperation. "Martin, we've only been going a few months. You can't expect to be catapulted into wealth, however well we do. If we aim for double the return you can get on a good savings account, we've done really well! The only way to get much higher returns is to take big risks, and by my estimate none of you can afford to lose what you've got invested here."

There was a general grunt of agreement.

"Look," K.P. continued "Do you know what the average annual return over 100-odd years the U.K. stock market has made, after inflation? It is less than six per cent, and most of it comes from re-investing dividends. If you're all thirsting for risk, why not start a separate portfolio just on paper, give yourselves ten million imaginary pounds and see how you do?"

"That's quite a good idea," said Harry. "Then I could say I'm a self-made paper millionaire. Then maybe even Chantelle would fall for me, wouldn't you, Darling?"

"In your dreams, Grandpa. And my nightmares."

As Harry agrees to get the next round in, I reflect that investment can be a laugh even when you're not making a bean.

Thursday 27th April: Heinkels over Isleworth

Drive around to Dot's as planned at 5pm. Had to park around the corner because the Victorian school opposite is in the process of demolition, and a JCB is half blocking the road. When I get to Dot's house I see the curtains are still drawn, local newspaper sticking out of the letterbox. No reply to doorbell. In something of a panic I use my own key to get in. I throw open the lounge door and put on the light. For half a second I think she's dead. Dot's legs, complete with zip-up slippers protrude from under the dining table.

"Have they gone, Geoffrey?" she whispers. It's always a bad one when she calls for my father, dead since 1988.

"Its me, Mum, Bernard. Are you alright? It looks very cosy!"

Under the table with her is a torch, a Thermos flask, the Radio Times and a collection of tinned fruit. She has walled one end of the table in with the sofa's seat cushions on their edge.

"Is it over? I didn't hear the All Clear," she rasps.

"There hasn't been a raid, Mum. I think it's the workmen opposite."

"Oh, there was a raid. Terrible noise from first thing. The whole street's got it, I expect. Didn't have time to tape the windows. Luckily, I've still got the Morrison."

Mum's Morrison shelter is actually a bleached pine economy table from Ikea, chosen because it's light enough for her to move. While the old oak heirloom she used to have may have boasted good anti-Luftwaffe credentials, this one wouldn't survive a direct hit from a meringue nest.

"It's alright Mum. They've demolished the old school. That's what you heard," I say gently.

"Oh they haven't! The poor, poor children. A direct hit, I expect."

"Mum, please. It's not been used since 1978. The war's been over for 60-odd years, look. It's 2006." I draw the curtains, and lead

92

her over to look. For a few seconds her face is a tapestry of wonder, as she absorbs the street scene as if for the first time.

"We won, then?"

"Of course we did," I say as I put the kettle on. "So have you been under there all day?"

"Since ten-to-eight. The house was shaking. It was awful."

"Well, it looks like they have done the noisy stuff. It should be quieter tomorrow."

Just when I think she's back with me in 2006 she throws me completely.

"Are we expecting a leaflet raid then?"

Tuesday 9th May: Keeping up with the Joneses

A moment I long dreaded. Went to Dot's to explain that Dad's share certificate in English Electric circa 1938 is now worth £600,000 and discuss the hurdles we need to cross to claim it. The full story is that EE was bought by GEC which largely went down a black hole called Marconi, all bar £593 worth which has washed up in a new firm called Telent, which is itself being dismembered. The real value is in another company, BAe Systems, which bought a chunk of GEC in 1999 and issued shares in payment. Getting our hands on the money will be just as tricky. The certificate is invalid, but if we can match Dad to a name and address on the register, we can claim. Trouble is, there are hundreds of Mr G. Jones there (curse of a common name.) Even if there's a match, additional identity checks will be needed, admin fees of £60 and hundreds of pounds for an indemnity from an insurance company to protect BAe (in case of what, I'm not sure). If the claim is established, a new nominee holding will be set up, and then the shares can be sold.

What I actually told her was this: "Mum, here's a special competition. If you can remember all Dad's addresses since 1938 we might be able to get some money. Quite a lot, actually."

The response was immediate. "Oh, I don't do competitions. Anyway, I've got enough here. I'm quite comfy."

Damn. She might be comfy, but what about me? I've got Eunice's credit card and conservatory habit to support. Clearly need to try another tack.

Elevenses: Excellent as always. Dot provided four cups of strong tea, plus two toasted teacakes with strawberry jam and clotted cream.

Wednesday 10th May: I told you so, at the Ring o'Bells

Arrived at the pub at 12.30pm for our usual fortnightly share club meeting. This time we deferred to Martin Gale, our Mondeo-driving 58-year-old civil engineer, who last month made a passionate case for investing in a tiddler called Fortune Oil when it was 5p. Since then it has briefly soared to 8.75p on news of a Chinese coal bed methane gas deal, and has now retreated to 6p.

"It's only going to be here for a week or two before shooting ahead!" he insists. "Let's buy now." K. P. Sharma shakes his head and insists this would be a speculation, pure and simple.

Harry Staines says, "Go on, give it a go, it's only a tanner a share. That's dirt cheap."

I am against, but don't admit the real reason which is that I haven't a clue about coal beds or methane reserves. Won't it just mean more dead canaries down the mine? Most interesting thing about the heated exchanges is the flecks of pork pie pastry that oscillate up and down on Martin's moustache. In the end he wins, with Harry and Mike Delaney's backing. Chantelle, the metal-studded gothic barmaid (today in black dress, black engineer's boots and red eyeshadow) is opposed. So is K.P. Sharma. I abstain. Chantelle, clearing the table as I leave says. "We've only got two investments, and they're both dependent on oil or metals. Ain't good, is it?"

Elevenses: The Bells has started doing a lunch menu. Warned off the scampi by Chantelle, I instead chose beef cobbler, at £6.99. Bad move, it's awful.

4pm: Peter Edgington has left a telephone message saying that he is off to Capri with the family, has sold most of his portfolio and finally: "The charts indicate shares are heading for a real pasting this summer. I should lighten up holdings on some of those dog stocks of yours Bernard, in all seriousness."

What an impertinent, overbearing and arrogant man! Rushed to the den to check the latest prices. All seems well (ish).

Thursday 11th May: Black widow rituals

Eunice's credit card bill would not disgrace Imelda Marcos. Seems last month's bunion emergency was merely a cloak to justify the complete renewal of her shoe collection. Nothing under sixty quid a pair! Doesn't she realise we have a conservatory to support? Then I notice £131.50 from Life Renewal Enterprises Inc, presumably that appalling life coach Josh Fenderbrun. Hadn't heard from him for a while, and hoped Eunice had got a refund. Prepared to tackle Eunice about it, with all the uneasiness of a male spider contemplating sex.

She turned on me in a second. "Bernard. If you want to waste your present that's up to you. Irmgard says Josh Fenderbrun is the best in the business, and she's shocked you were so rude to him. They won't refund, so you may as well get some use from it."

Friday 12th May: Edgington vindicated

Stock market fell out of bed! Sat at the keyboard at breakfast, munching on toast and honey, and amazed to see all those red numbers. What on earth is happening? Didn't have much chance to mull it over, because I have to find a birthday present for my monster grandson Digby, who will be eight a week today. Phoned Janet for some hints for what to buy. Forget hints, the woman has a detailed list that wouldn't disgrace a society wedding: X-Box console, mountain bike, new skateboard, some very specific kind of training shoes (In fact so specific that she said she and Brian would purchase them to make sure they weren't somehow 'wrong'. That baffled me. So long as they fit, how can they be wrong?)

"What about books?" I asked, hoping to keep under £20.

"Well, of course we do encourage him to read. But it isn't easy to get his interest."

"What about Harry Potter? Everyone likes Harry Potter," I said, particularly thinking of K.P. Sharma at the share club who bought 1,000 shares in publisher Bloomsbury long before J. K. Rowling had even discovered Jobseekers Allowance.

"Yes, he's been through most of them," Janet responded. "They just don't tend to last. *Harry Potter and Prisoner of Azkaban* got trapped behind the spin dryer and had its cover torn off, *Harry Potter and the Philosopher's Stone* Digby traded for a novelty cigarette lighter and a packet of condoms, while *Harry Potter and the Half Blood Prince* was left behind in the gents at Scratchwood services at Easter during one of Digby's vomiting attacks."

"A packet of condoms!"

"Oh, it's not like that. He's no interest in girls yet, thank God. No, the kids use them for water bombs, mainly. They also put yoghurt in them, and leave them on…."

"Alright, let's forget books. What about Lego?"

"Ooh no, he's going to be eight. It really isn't the same anymore. His generation think Lego is for children, he'll want something they regard as cool."

Giving up, I told Janet that I had few ideas of my own. I hope Digby likes surprises.

Chapter Ten

Riding the Correction

Monday 15th May: Plunging markets

Good God, the market's in freefall! Over 100 points down on the FTSE. I could strangle Peter Edgington for being such a know-all. I really don't understand this nonsense about inflation worries. Why now? Inflation is about two per cent. That's nothing! In 1975, I recall it was 24 per cent. Now *that* was an inflation worry. Seems they don't even make economic crises like they used to. Dither over my portfolio, already down £3,400 since Thursday. Perhaps I should sell something. But what if it recovers?

Elevenses: Big slice of treacle tart.

Close of play: Market has halved its losses. Notice Hornby's keeping up the momentum after those fantastic results last month. I do wish I'd bought more. Actually, even Compass is doing okay down 2p. The advantage of dogs – they can only be beaten down so far.

Tuesday 16th May: Better late than never

Compass interim results. With the restatements and exclusions it's hard to make head or tail of them, but at least the shares picked up to around 240p. Interrupted at 8.45am by builders arriving en-masse, with digger. This is the Medway team apparently, led by that annoying gnome with a clipboard. He soon disappears and the rest set to work on the foundations for the damn conservatory. Digger is present for all of two minutes before reversing over Eunice's geraniums. Skip is moved into back garden, this time it's friendly fire on her delphiniums. I intervene before they get the clematis. "Sorry mate, thought they wuz weeds." Moronic peasants!

Trying to concentrate on the market, which is yo-yoing horribly. Could already be too late to sell, even Spirent which is down 20 per cent from its recent peak of nearly 50p.

Elevenses: Hornby drawer key seems to have disappeared from the hook above my PC in the den. This is annoying. I've got an unopened packet of six fondant fancies in there, picked up from the Kwik Save discount bin last week.

Close of play: Market seems to have steadied at 5850. Thank God that's over! Glad I didn't bother to sell. Should all be upward from here.

Wednesday 17th May - Humbug and humous

Equitable life AGM today, but I can't bear to go just to hear some depressing humbug. Would be worse than remaining here, where builders' noise is driving me mad.

Elevenses: Still can't find the key. Nothing edible in entire house. In fridge found a tub of something which looked like tile grout, labelled 'humous'. Olives, pitta breads, Waitrose falafel. Not a fan of such nosh, but Eunice is making a big effort because Irmgard and her so-called 'partner' Nils, a media training consultant, are coming for dinner tonight. Why can't they just admit to being common law husband and wife? That's what the local paper still calls them in its reports from the magistrate's court: 'Potter admitted he hit his common law wife, but claimed he was provoked after she claimed she was bored of hearing about Wayne Rooney's injured metatarsal.'

Close of Play: Market's plunged again! Down another £4,370 after Wall Street slide. A week ago we were at 6,100 on the FTSE, now we're back at 5,650. What timing that Alan Greenspan had leaving when he did. Looks like the new Fed chap Bernanke's getting it in the neck already.

Dinner party: Oh what JOY. Global warming, recycling and animal liberation. Irmgard has an earnest view on anything, and as much sense of humour as a Saudi executioner. She berated Eunice for buying Chilean grapes which are flown here, but earlier had boasted that her disgusting Fairtrade guanaco fluff poncho was made by Peruvian villagers. So how did it get to the UK then? Perhaps it crawled.

Eunice flirted endlessly with Nils, who with his tight black rollneck and blond hair looked to me like Dr No's bodyguard. Afterwards Eunice claimed he was 'dishy', and went on endlessly (while I did the washing up) about his ice-blue eyes. I did concur that he, or indeed any sighted male, would be a catch for the spaniel-faced harridan, but got flicked with a tea towel for my trouble.

Midnight postscript: After bedtime harangue have finally agreed to meet this damn life coach Josh Fenderbrun. Anything for a bit of peace!

Friday 19th May: In for a pounding

I woke up with a cracking headache, probably brought on by last night's meal with Mike Delaney at the Koh-I-Noor, where I mixed Kingfisher lager, prawn dhansak and a double Drambuie. The first two would surely have been fine, but there is some part of the human brain which goaded by alcohol always oversteps the mark: "How about a double jeroboam of monkey brain cordial, Sir?"

"Oh, yes go on, why not?" is what we reply. In for a penny, in for a cerebral pounding. Ibuprofen cannot shift this anvil of hate riding in my temple. Today is the eighth birthday of my grandson, Digby. Not wholly coincidentally, it is also the birthday of Pol Pot. As I hobble into the den to look at shares, I have a sense of foreboding. The dark forces of the universe are clearly in astrological alliance, and I can even feel the black hole of wickedness pull on my portfolio where value is seeping out at an alarming rate. Once shares disappear over the event horizon they are lost for ever. If astronomers ever decide that black holes exist, I shall propose they name the first three Jarvis, Railtrack and Equitable Life.

Elevenses: A cup-a-soup, lovingly prepared by that Escoffier of convenience, Eunice who assured me it would help settle my stomach. Stuff looked and tasted vile enough, then I made the cardinal error of looking at the packet: glucose syrup, hydrogenated vegetable oil, ammonia caramel, beta carotene and dipotassium phosphate, E471, E621, E635. I ran to the loo and was sick with ease.

Saturday 20ᵗʰ May: Key reversal

Though Digby doesn't play with Lego, we still thought a trip to Legoland would make a nice outing with all of its marvellous scale models. Why don't I ever learn? Brian and Janet drove the Antichrist over to us by 9.30am, and together with a relentlessly miserable Jemima we packed into the Volvo. Having set out at 11.40am in brilliant sunshine, only an hour and forty minutes later than planned, we hit the M25 and solid traffic from junction six. Nothing moved for an hour, but the overhead signs taunted us by continually flashing 60mph. 'Ha-ha-ha. Here's a speed you can't do'. It could hardly be more irritating if they had electronic mooning.

So what was the cause? The traffic news on the radio told us about road works anti -clockwise at junction 18, a broken down car in the Dartford Tunnel, and a lorry which had shed its load of toilet seats at Apex Corner on the North Circular. About what was delaying us, an instant overheated refugee camp of thousands without food, water or information, there was not a word. Only one thing could make the experience worse:

"Mum, I need to go to the toilet."

"Oh, Digby, you choose your moments," said Janet.

"Which is it, Digby?" Brian whispered.

"What?"

"It is number ones or number twos?" he hissed. We all groaned when we heard the reply.

"Digby, We're in the fast lane. You can't just nip out. I'm sorry but you'll just have to wait," I said.

"But I *have* been waiting!" he wailed. "For a whole hour! And I need to go now."

"Alright," said Brian. "I'll go with him. There's some bushes on top of the embankment. We're not going anywhere for a while are we?" Brian let Digby out, ferreted around in the boot for whatever health and safety equipment he needed, and they threaded their way past a Tesco lorry and a BOC gas bottle truck across to the hard shoulder and up into the bushes.

After five minutes they still hadn't returned. Looking far ahead, I could see vehicle brake lights going off.

"Oh God, they're moving," I said.

The wave of movement advanced towards us.

"Come on, Digby, come on," wailed Janet, but there was still no sign of them.

"I'll have to move, I'm afraid," I said.

"Bernard, you will not abandon my son and grandson in their hour of need," said Eunice shielding the handbrake with her hand. "Why don't you edge right to the crash barrier?"

"That's no help, is it! When traffic gets back up to eighty they won't be able to cross three lanes of traffic!"

Behind us, someone in a mirror-filling BMW 4x4 leant on the horn and edged to within a whisker of the boot. There was a 100 yard gap in front of me and already the middle lane was up to 30 mph. I set off, but it took me five minutes, and goodness knows how many miles to force my way across three lanes to the hard shoulder. Putting the car into reverse, and with hazards lights on, I edged the Volvo backwards. Trouble was, I had no idea how far I had to go. For ten very slow minutes I crawled backwards.

"Is this right, anyone?" I asked.

"I think it's too far," said Janet.

"No, they were much further back, by those yellow flowers," Eunice said.

"They're not flowers, that's ragwort," said Jemima, the first words of any kind to pass her lips all day. "And it kills horses."

"Thank you for your contribution," I said. "Now, bright ideas anyone?"

"Has Brian got his phone with him?" Eunice said, wielding her own.

"Damn, it's here," Janet said. "Aah, but Digby will have his."

Finally connected to Brian, we heard that they had to walk across two minor roads and a field to get any seclusion. They claimed they were now on the ridge of the embankment, but we couldn't see them, and there were no obvious landscape features to navigate by.

"What big lorries can you see?" I asked.

"There's a Sainsbury lorry just level with us in the slow lane."

After waiting two minutes no such lorry had passed us, so we reckoned we must have come too far in reverse. Finally, we found them, and there was much rejoicing.

"Feeling better now?" I asked a dejected looking Digby.

"Couldn't go."

"What!!!"

Brian had only one word of explanation. "Wind."

Tuesday 23rd May: Qinetiq lethargy

Good God, the market's down near 5,500! I thought it was all over last week, but now who knows where it will go? Sold Bovis at 760p while I still had some profits (about 100p per share). Drives me mad! Could have sold at 940p at the end of March. Qinetiq down to 170p, which is a 20 per cent loss. What on earth has this market turmoil got to do with the multi-year-contracts business of a defence technology firm?

Elevenses: Used screwdriver to break open the Hornby drawer. Broke lock and gashed thumb. Bugger! Got blood all over last month's *Railway Modeller*. The fondant fancies are gone. This is sabotage and has to stop.

Chapter Eleven

Heavy Breathing

Thursday 1ˢᵗ June: Who dares, whinges

Market seems to be recovering a little. Only made back £1,300 of worst losses, and Qinetiq and Spirent seem immovably weak. Having sold Bovis at 760p it has now recovered to 835p. Damn and blast! Perhaps I was wrong to sell. Bought them back at 840p, which turned out to be the day's peak. That's 800 quid up the swanny.

Finally got my mother to remember some addresses where she and my father lived. Have e-mailed them off to Telent and BAe registrars.

Elevenses: Asked Eunice if she knew where my Hornby drawer key had got to. "Isn't it on the car key ring?" No, of course not I respond, but then there it is. I'm sure I didn't put it there. Tackled about the missing fondant fancies, Eunice feigns ignorance. After having broken the lock last week, I'm stuck once again with no privacy.

Friday 2ⁿᵈ June: Yorkshire terror

Doorbell rings at 7.15am. Put on dressing gown. Grumble on way downstairs, assume it is unusually early start from builders. Open door to see beefy grinning fellow in athletic gear, noisily chewing gum. "Good morning B'nard. Are you ready to greet the day?"

"Oh God, it isn't...."

"Yes, that's right. Josh Fenderbrun. You'll soon be glad you changed your mind."

"I didn't. My wife changed my mind. Good God man, do you know what the time is?" I had recalled the dreaded life coach was coming today, but had assumed it would be some civilised time.

"Early starts, always. It's all on the documentation, B'nard. Haven't you prepared yourself for module 1? Did you watch the video?"

"Look. I did agree to see you, but I haven't had time to watch the video or anything."

"Okay, today, B'nard is a two hour introductory session about breathing. Br-e-e-e-athing," he said, exhaling a nasty waft of spearmint into my face. "Open your body to oxygen, open your mind to relaxation. He then asked me if I had my 'jogging suit' and 'sneakers' ready. It gradually dawned on me that exercise of some sort was involved. After some acrimonious exchanges, I left him on the doorstep and went upstairs, returning in moleskin trousers, Barbour jacket and stout brogues.

His jaw dropped. "We're not going on safari, B'nard." He's equally shocked that not only do I not belong to a gym, but that I don't know where the nearest one is. We agree to go to the park half a mile away, and then I'm shocked when he goes to unlock his car. "Aren't we going to walk?" I say.

"Is it safe?" he asks.

"It's north Kent, not Chechnya!"

On arrival at the park, I watch in embarrassed awe as he starts running on the spot, bellowing instructions and flinging his arms wide. I decline to participate, merely watching as joggers and dog walkers stare slack-jawed at this testosterone twit hurling his body into the air.

"C'mon B'nard, jump, get with it," he boomed. "Get those quads into action."

At this moment a Yorkshire terrier comes tearing over yipping wildly, chased by an elderly lady. The diminutive hound circles Fenderbrun, nipping at his ankles and finally sinking its teeth into his tracksuit.

"Naughty Titus, stop it!" the lady says, adding for Fenderbrun's benefit: "I'm so sorry, but you Americans are too tanned. Titus just assumed you were a coloured person."

The session fizzles out, with Fenderbrun wiping dog saliva from his ankles and me bent double gasping for breath, stomach muscles aching. Haven't laughed so much for years. He says he'll come next Friday, and I'm too winded to argue.

Elevenses: Two gorgeous fresh cream éclairs from the local bakers. Feel I've earned them with all this exercise.

Close of play. Market recovered quite nicely. Notice Prescott, Jemima's enormous suede pig has now been installed in the den. It looks as glum as the deputy prime minister.

Wednesday 7th June: General samosas

Awful day. Market fallen sharply again. Bovis has now fallen under 800p! I seem to be like a reverse trader. Buy high, sell low. How utterly depressing. How long is this going to go on? That chap who runs the Fidelity fund, Anthony Bolton, seems to think it may last all summer. Well, that's all right for him, he's leaving. What about the rest of us?

To cap it all Qinetiq came in with some fairly miserable results. Profits down, just a few months after the IPO! Business with the MoD has halved, and the staff are up in arms for more pay too. I've lost 15 per cent since February. Decided not to mention it any more at share club.

Elevenses: Mrs Sharma's samosas, distributed by K.P. at the Ring o'Bells. He said they were mild, but one bite almost sent me to Pluto. By God we didn't half drink some beer afterwards. The drunken recriminations about Billiton purchase, already below £10 ("We should have bought it cheaper," says Martin Gale, master of the obvious) are followed by misery that we don't yet have enough cash to make a new purchase. Gale also suggested we open a spread-betting account to gear up our remaining pittance. Firmly rejected. The man's a loose cannon.

Tuesday 13th June: Dead cat bounce

Tokyo stock market took a whack this morning. Knew it must be bad when they mentioned it on Radio 4's Today programme, which doesn't normally give a fig about business or markets. Ran to the den, tripping over the bloody cat, which I rather unceremoniously ejected into the garden. Sure enough, from the opening bell FTSE 100 dropped out of the bottom of the trading range to below 5,500. Everything's down! This is awful. I'd promised to make enough money by April to pay for the conservatory, but have merely lost enough to buy a small car.

9.45am. Ring on doorbell. Eunice forget her keys? Maybe the builders, now AWOL for a week, have decided to resume work? Not so. A big 4x4, four way flashers on, is parked at the front, and a woman is standing on the doorstep in the rain looking rather sheepish. "Did you have a black and white cat?" she says. "Because I'm afraid…"

Did? Oh God, Hermès! I rush out and inspect. The tail looks about right, but…well, for the rest all I can tell is that it was once a cat. Huge guilt that I forced the poor animal out to its death. Woman departs after a thousand apologies, (and flashers still on, daft bat). Must get sorted before Eunice returns. I shovel the remains into a Waitrose bag (only the best, you know). Pour sand on the gory stains in the road. Dig a hole at bottom of garden behind cucumber frames, gently deposit Hermès and pat earth on top. Fashion a crude wooden cross from old fruit box (getting splinter and banging thumb with hammer), and am just starting to think about some appropriately maudlin words when I hear Eunice's car. She is inconsolable.

Elevenses: Take Eunice out to lunch at La Pergola, money and wine no object. Lots of snivelling. On our return she rallies enough to inflict a hippopotamus manoeuvre on me, knowing I can hardly refuse. First in the afternoon, surely, since Ian Smith declared UDI.

Close of play: Markets panned. Sit in the den watching Wall Street's miserable close. Long shot: used remaining spread-bet credit for a modest up bet on the Nasdaq at 2075. Jemima arrives home from work at 10.30pm. More cat-related waterworks.

Wednesday 14th June: Spirent spirals

Lie awake listening to Eunice's broken drain impersonation, and worrying about shares. Decide this is lunacy and get up. Walk into kitchen and in the dawn light see a cat outside. Not any cat, but our cat. Whoop with delight, scoop up the feline and race upstairs to show Eunice. Only having dropped purring puss on bed and woken the trouble-and-strife do I recall it is 4.20am. Still, I'm soon forgiven.

8am. Profit warning from Spirent. Shares 45p yesterday, 36p today. Bang head on wall. I'm cursed! Why didn't I sell? Now I can't, I've lost too much. Worst of all, I still don't understand what this blood company does. Problem arose in 'Performance analysis broadband' due to lower sales of 'older platforms' and transition to newer 'product solutions.' I'm none the wiser, quite honestly.

Elevenses: Hot crumpet with melted butter and strawberry jam. Fantastic, took me right back to childhood. However, caught in the act by Eunice who returned early from shopping (I'd assumed she was going to Bluewater).

"Bernard, I think we need to have a talk about your food secrets." The lecture starts on the five a day vegetable portion, moves on to my health (cholesterol, age, exercise, possibility of diabetes), and then to my "secretive habits."

"What do you mean secretive?"

"This drawer you used to hide food in. And that silly tunnel on your railway, that I found jam tarts in the other week." How did she know about that?

"Bernard, you have to realise that if you put sticky sweet things in the loft, I'll be able to smell them when I collect your tea mugs."

Good grief. The woman's got a nose like a truffle-hunting pig.

Friday 16th June: Coach and hearses

Josh Fenderbrun arrives at 8am. We agree that if I find exercise embarrassing, I can do it indoors. He starts me at the foot of the stairs, doing step-ups. Then going up two stairs and down and then three. All the time this booming voice is in my ear: "Breathe B'nard, use those lungs. Stop wheezing." To wind down after the 'workout' I'm told to lie on the floor and think of nothing, but all I can visualise is my portfolio, disappearing down a whirlpool. This isn't hugging the inner me, it's suffocating it. Subsequent sessions, thank God, will take place by phone.

Elevenses: One orange, peeled and prepared by Eunice who supervises my medication like Nurse Ratched from *One Flew Over the Cuckoo's Nest.*

7pm: Am reading and re-reading the Spirent annual report, hoping for some ray of light in the misery of my losses when doorbell goes. Two angelic little girls of about seven are standing there, with some crayoned posters in their hands. "Have you seen our cat?" they ask. "He's called Snuggles and he's black and white."

Chapter Twelve

In for a Penny, In for a Pound

Wednesday 21ˢᵗ June: Penny stocks, pounding losses
Sat outside at the Ring o'Bells for the share club meeting, soaking up this rare heat. However, the club portfolio is clearly wilting. Billiton, bought at £11.55 is still down to £10 or so. Fortune Oil, the brainchild of Martin Gale, our very own speculator, was bought at 6.5p, and the price now is 5.8p. It's actually worse than that, as K.P. Sharma rightly pointed out. The spread is at least a halfpenny, so we could only get 5.5p if we sold now. That 1p fall is a 15% loss. Thank goodness we could only afford to buy 4,000 of them in the first place. With little cash in the kitty for new investments, and losses already behind us, the mood was a little glum. All except Harry Staines who, despite being 73, eyed every passing woman.

"Phwoar, look at those," he said of one buxom brunette. "Two and half British standard handfuls there, I'd reckon."

K.P. Sharma, born in India and brought up in colonial Uganda, raised a quizzical eyebrow at the mention of this hitherto undiscovered imperial unit.

"Don't ask," I said. "You'll regret it."

Elevenses: My share of two large packets of cracked pepper kettle crisps while Mike Delaney and Harry earnestly discussed Iran vs Angola. God! I'm so sick of the World Cup.

Close of play: Up £112. Nasdaq Composite up-bet, placed at 2075 on May 13th, clearly in profit at 2120. Market does seem to be gradually recovering.

Thursday 22nd June: Bernard's lost notes

Eunice has tidied up the den and now I can't half find my notes. Yesterday's close of play prices. Gone. Detailed notes on the food companies I'm researching. Gone. I had compared Britvic, Northern Foods and Premier Foods, and had written down all their yields and P/E ratios. Gone. The only thing that is still there is bloody Prescott, the suede pig, sitting on my chair with his trotters on the PC keyboard. Perhaps he should do the investing. Can't be any worse at it than I am.

"I know not to throw things away, Bernard," Eunice responds when I ask her. "But why don't you buy a proper pad of paper. It's inevitable that you'll lose things written on envelopes. Don't you remember that time you'd written the electronic ticket reservation number for our flight to Malta on the household insurance renewal which I was sending back to the Pru? We nearly missed the plane!"

Elevenses: A handful of grapes and a banana, no doubt placed in the Hornby drawer by 'matron'.

Friday 23rd June: Coach party

7.15am. Life coach Fenderbrun rings just as I'm emerging from the shower. Wants to discuss how the 'Inner B'nard' is evolving. I tell him the outer me is clean but wet, and thanks to Eunice the inner me is overdosed on exotic fruit, nuts and other jungle junk. The only evolving I'm likely to do is growing a prehensile tail.

Elevenses: A banana, half of which was bad.

11pm. Eunice is dropped back after from some drinks party for the basket weaving set. She's drunk, again. Claims to be on a special Pimms diet. So far she's lost two days.

Saturday 24th June: A vision in beige

Jemima seems v. depressed. Every telephone conversation with former boyfriend Toby (several per evening) gets the waterworks going. "Why do you keep calling him if it upsets you?" I had the temerity to ask.

Eunice tugged me into the kitchen. "For goodness sake Bernard, leave here alone. You're so insensitive."

"I'm not."

"Yes you *are*. Remember when she was going to marry Tymon…"

"Oh, yes that *awful* split-capital trust salesman…"

"She came in wearing her wedding dress to show you. And do you remember what you said?"

"Yes. I pronounced her a 'delightful vision in beige'. And she was."

"Bernard, you are hopeless. No wonder she burst into tears. Beige is a horrible, dowdy middle-aged colour."

"So why did she order a dress in it?"

"She didn't. It was soft ivory, for goodness sake!"

"It doesn't matter what it said on the label, it was bloody beige. And it cost £1,250! And it had to go back when we discovered Tymon was rogering an aromatherapist from Bromley! I'm sorry, Eunice, Jem has to stop being so bloody soppy."

Eunice's final word? "Oh, go up and play with your train set."

Tuesday 27th June: Martin Gale in action

Slightly sheepish phone call from Martin about his own shares. He bought a £6,000 holding in iSoft in January at 390p having read about it in a tip sheet. After this huge profit warning in February, they plummeted to 180p. Confident of recovery, he doubled up, taking out a £6,000 loan again his house equity. He says: "I would have broken even at 285p, that was the attraction. But now they're down at 70p. You're a safety-first man, Bernard. What would you do?"

I tell him I'd buy a box of fresh cream éclairs and eat the lot.

Thursday 29th June: FTSE leads the way

Huge rise in FTSE, over 100 points! Finally, it looks like this correction is giving up the ghost. Good rises across the board, barring Spirent of course, which seems on a relentless slide. Decide to forget that I paid 82p for them in 2004 and sell anyway. Get just 37p a share, loss of £4,500. Awful.

Elevenses: Sneaked in a plain chocolate Bounty. If the gastronomic Gestapo catch me, I shall explain that it was the coconut filling I was after. If ketchup is one of the five portions a day, then surely this is.

Close of play: Up £3,816. The up-bet on the Nasdaq is now showing a 5% profit, so I'll take it. That's £2 a point, £200.

Friday 30th June: Yank the chain

8am. Good early start. Finally found my notes on Britvic, Premier Foods and Northern Foods. Low P/Es, decent yields, but what of the outlook? Just getting to grips with details when life coach Fenderbrun rings. Tedious questions. No, I haven't watched the damn video. No, I haven't read his tedious book. No, I haven't done any more damn silly exercises.

"Well, B'nard," he sighs. "You do seem to have a bunch of attitudinal issues which I think we ought to progress towards a resolution timeline. I'm coming to visit with you next time."

"I'll arrange not to be in, then," I say as I hang up.

Elevenses: The corduroy hand grenades have reappeared in the drawer. Still, perhaps I should save these kiwis to hurl at Fenderbrun when he comes next week.

6pm. Get a phone call from Martin Gale. Says he's made a smart investment on behalf of the club. "Now the World Cup's over, I've just laid hands on 26 boxes of England car flags for just 37p a pair, compared to £1.79 full retail. All we need to do is keep them to the next UEFA Euro championship in 2008, and we'll all make a killing."

"Where are you going to store them?"

"Ah, yes. I was just getting to that. You know that conservatory of yours…"

No, no and no!

Saturday 1st July: Re-education camp

Took Eunice and Jem over for tea with Brian, Janet and the Antichrist. Arrive to discover my schoolteacher son is having a 'house stakeholders meeting'. Janet discovered a mobile phone in Digby's jacket, stolen from another child. The pocket-sized Satan claims it was given to him. Brian, rather than give the imp the good hiding he so richly deserves, has fallen back on Vietnamese re-education techniques. While Janet takes notes, Brian tells his son in moderated Mandelson-like tones that they are seeking a 'paradigm shift' in his behaviour.

"We don't mind you taking the phone, Digby. We don't really. But the dishonesty is very hurtful to Janet and to me as household leader."

Meanwhile the child chants 'Look bogies!' and holds back his nostrils, gleefully displaying the vile contents of his head to all concerned.

"He's got attention deficit disorder with hyperactivity, poor mite," explains Janet.

Eunice's fixes me with a glare which says: Bernard, don't you dare say anything. Over tea, the tiny tyrant, far from being clapped in irons, beeps away at a Gameboy and noisily sucks a litre carton of chocolate milk through a straw. So much for punishment.

Monday 3rd July: BAe ringmaster at Airbus circus

Only a bunch of clowns would make an aircraft with a Spanish tailfin, a German fuselage, British wings, and glued together by the French. Oh dear, the A380 doesn't fit together. Profit warning, angry customers. Only then does BAe confirm it wants to sell its share in Airbus, using a valuation (that it commissioned itself!) which says its stake is worth 20% less than it wanted. What a circus! And we poor shareholders have paid the admission price.

3pm. Builders finally finish off the conservatory roof. All that is left are the door handles and fittings to be re-ordered from China, because Eunice spotted the last ones were 'brass effect' not the gold she ordered. Could have saved £370 plus VAT if we'd accepted them, but oh no, we had to go the whole hog.

Friday 7th July: Vic and the vixen

7.15am. Went out for a constitutional to avoid the dreaded life coach and his irritating early morning phone calls that besmirch my Fridays. Marvellous sunny morning, park deserted so strolled over to the hill-top bench and (once discarded pizza box removed) sat to soak up the view of mist-laden beeches in the valley beneath. The sun glinting off the stream silhouetted a heron as it descended on unhurried wings for an early stickleback or two. My reverie was soon disturbed. Along the path was ambling a stocky fellow in an old and shiny gabardine mac, with florid face and a shock of greasy grey hair. The final giveaway was the four filthy Sainsbury bags looped on a string over his shoulder.

"Mind if I sit down, Governor?"

"Help yourself," I replied, though in truth the bench was not as long as I would have liked.

"I've sat here every morning for over 12 years," he said, revealing a carious grin.

"Really?"

"Yes. That's the life of Vic Handley. Nineteen years in the Royal Navy for queen and country, six years with the Peninsular & Oriental Steam Navigation Company and twelve years here on the brow of Finnstead Fields."

He reached into a bag and pulled out a bottle of Magners cider. Unscrewing the top, he peered inside. It was half empty. He took a small swig, and then paused before offering me the bottle. "Sorry, Governor. Would you like a drop yourself?"

"No, thanks."

He puzzled for a second, the muttered an apology. He wiped the grime-blackened cuff of his mac vigorously over the bottle top. "That's better. Must remember me manners." He waved the newly buffed bottle toward me.

Trying to suppress my gag reflex, I raised a cautionary hand.

"I've got a hangover from last night," I lied.

"I don't get them any more," Vic said. "Still get drunk, mind. But no hangovers. I've no place left to have the pain in, what with all me dead brain cells. That's what me wife reckoned."

"Your wife?"

"Yeah. Alice. Childhood sweetheart. She got the house, the kids, the car, all that in 1973."

"When you divorced?"

He nodded. "Not seen me kids for 20 years. They moved away. Besides, they'd all be grown now, with families of their own. Still, it don't matter. Not when you got all this to look at every morning. Amazing. No-one sees the dawn any more. I mean, really looks at the colours, the shape of the clouds. At five in the morning there's no-one here to see it but me. Even by eight almost everyone else is all rushing about, ferrying kids, jumping in cars and what not."

"True. No time to stand and stare."

"That was written by a tramp," Vic said.

"Really? I had no idea," I said, hiding my scepticism.

"You know, in all this there's only one thing I miss."

"What's that?"

"My old Garrard record player. She got that too. Here look," he said, delving into one of his bags. He pulled out a scuffed record still in its sleeve. "I've got all my old Billie Holiday '78s, but nowhere to play 'em. Now that's a shame ain't it?"

"They must be worth a bit now," I said. "Have you been carrying them about like this for 12 years?"

"Reckon so. They've become good friends now. I couldn't sell them. Besides, money's not important to me. I've got what I need."

"Where do you sleep?"

"Different places. There's a wooden bus shelter down at Heligoland Road, but I sometimes get moved on. In summer, when it's dry, I sleep in the woods there. I only get disturbed by the vixen, and she knows me now. We're like old mates. I bring her the boxes from my KFC chicken dinners, and she'll take 'em from my hand now."

After another half an hour, and almost reluctantly, I took my leave of Vic. While I could neither sleep rough nor drink cider for breakfast, I realised I had just got a valuable bit of life coaching. And it was free.

Monday 10th July: V or W, £600,000 question

Mum phones to say she has received a letter she doesn't understand. Of course, she rarely understands any of her post, but this letter turns out to be from Telent's share registrars. Inevitably (and in some excitement) I have to drive round to Isleworth to look at it myself. It turns out there is a match on one of the addresses she provided to the old GEC share register that Telent has. The last contact was back in the late 1960s. However, instead of my father's actual initials, G. V. Jones, it is down as G. W. Jones. The letter asks Dot to somehow show that these are the same people. How on earth are we going to do that? Perhaps we can prove that our Geoffrey Victor Jones did live at 63, Downland Terrace, but how do we prove that someone called G. W. Jones never did? Hugely frustrating: £600,000 riding on one typing error.

Chapter Thirteen

Bat out of Hell

Wednesday 12 July: FTSE leads the way

FTSE going sideways again, can't seem to reach 5,900. Been like this for a few days. Still feeling a bit more optimistic, until I hear that Lebanon is flaring up again. What will this do for oil prices, I wonder?

Share club at the Ring o'Bells, and at last we have a few hundred to spend. Mike Delaney argues that we should wait until it's a thousand for an economic holding, and there's general agreement. Chantelle, today sporting pink hair, is serving behind the bar, but shouts across that we should go for something that won't "wobble with the price of oil". Have to admit that the two existing stocks have done exactly that. Not much of a portfolio, if everything moves together.

K.P. Sharma suggested we should have a 'theme' discussion, each arguing the corner for a person who embodied a powerful brand. Martin Gale went for Richard Branson ("Made personal service matter"), Mike Delaney went for Nelson Mandela ("The Teflon Terrorist"), and I went for Delia Smith, patron saint of traditional cooking. Harry Staines went for Raquel Welch, though seemed to miss the point, but Chantelle had the best: David Attenborough. We had to agree that if he launched a range of environmentally-friendly foods or garden products he'd make a mint.

Get back at 3pm to find Eunice has taken to her bed with a migraine. Still, she's well enough to give me a vast to-do list. Laundry. Vacuuming. Waitrose. Buy card for Dot's birthday on Tuesday. It goes on and on, with sub-clauses and sub-lists for each category. E.g. Waitrose: "Wholemeal fusilli pasta (not farfalle), honey roast ham from the counter, (not packet) etc, etc. She's clearly taken the opportunity to dump a whole week's housework on me.

Close of Play: Exhausted by this shopping business. Quick glance at FTSE shows it sagged late on, just as I have.

Thursday 13th July: Shopper's revenge

8am. News shows footage of huge Israeli reprisals on Lebanon for Hezbollah capture of two soldiers. Bridges, factories, roads, apartment blocks. Loads of civilian deaths. God, this is awful. Feel guilty for thinking about portfolio at such a time. Can't think it affects anything directly, but share prices are weaker all round. Even defence firms BAe and Qinetiq, weirdly enough.

Reprisals aren't confined to Middle East. Eunice, bounces out of bed in a foul mood. No thanks offered to yours truly for yesterday's efforts: I got the wrong pasta, the wrong ham, not enough kiwis (one), the laundry was left in the machine overnight (do I have to remember everything?), I didn't vacuum the en-suite properly because she can see there's floss on the floor, and to cap it all I didn't wind the bloody Dyson cable the correct way. "Bernard, this is why women are never ill," she tells me. "They have to do it all again the next day."

Elevenses: Two Waitrose chocolate cup cakes. Ha ha ha! Who says I got the wrong food. There's a carrier bag in the garage, and it's full of chocolate muffins, crisps, eccles cakes, and a tin of spotted dick.

Close of play: Market weaker again. Oh Lord, I'm getting seasick staring at the screen. What is the point? Made me think of Friday's sit down in the park. 'What is this life, if full of care, We have no time to stand and stare.' Looked the poem up. Smelly Vic was right. It was written by a tramp. William Davies, 1871-1940.

Thursday 14th July: The bloody O'Riordans

Eurotunnel looks like it will be disappearing up its own dark passageway shortly. Glad I never had shares in it, but as I recall Peter so-bloody-perfect Edgington did, just so he could get a discount going to his chateau in the Gironde. Funny he never brags about that investment. Best thing about it now is that almost all the shareholders left from the umpteenth refinancing are French. Perhaps I am getting old and bitter. Eunice called me a xenophobe the other day. "I'm certainly not, I replied. "My disdain is shared equally amongst all races, creeds and colours, regardless of disability, age, socio-economic grouping, size and sexual orientation." I suppose that makes me a misanthrope, the most politically correct of all old miseries.

Case in point. Gorgeous weather. Sat in garden until driven out by the O'Riordan's music. Two huge speakers on their patio blasting out gibberish (rat music, I think it's called, perfect for those vermin next door) but no-one actually listening, even if it could be understood. They only moved in six months ago, but its already turning into a council estate. Ken's a 'residential developer' from Essex, but clearly just a jumped-up builder. His skinny bottle-blonde wife Lisa (number two apparently) has a voice like a band saw and arrived pre-packaged with three vile, screechy, ginger kids. Bethany, 15, is already a little trollop with a pierced navel and language that would shock a Millwall supporter. Then there's Liam, 12, a hyperactive dimwit who worships David Beckham, but who can only 'bend it' into my bloody greenhouse. Finally there's a snivelling child of four who seems to be called You Little Tosser. For God's sake we know these people exist, but why do they have to have money? That house went for £425,000! Oh, I so regret Dr and Mifanwy Davies moving out, even though we fell out about my leylandii hedge. I feel we've been cursed. Bloody Welsh!

Friday 15ᵗʰ July: Slow coach
7.30am. Life coach Josh Fenderbrun, the world's most irritating person, rings up and asks me to describe the progress I have made in 'hugging the inner me'.

"The major progress so far is controlling my temper with you. There's actually nothing wrong with my self regard. It's you I find difficulty with. Your absurd exercise ideas, your silly epithets and corporate mumbo jumbo over all these weeks of our unfortunate and extended acquaintance haven't really changed anything except the relative sizes of our respective bank balances."

"Wow, B'nard. I have to say that your are my most challenging client, period. Your refusal, even after all these weeks to get with the programme, to overview the visual aids I provided or eyeball the documentation make it seriously challenging to get you to engage with the Inner You philosophy. Don't despair though, B'nard. I rise to a challenge, however difficult."

"Slow learning seems to go in both directions. Time and time again, Mr Fenderbrun, I have requested that you pronounce my name properly. It is BERnud not BerNARD."

"Got it. Brrrrrnud. Brrrrrnud."

"Yes, very good. But would you mind practising in your own time? I'm not paying for an open-ended course in teaching Americans how to speak." At which point I replaced the receiver.

Elevenses: Half a lemon and lime jaffa cake, purchased in a colossal two-for-the-price-of-one error from the discount bin at Kwik Save. I don't like lemon and lime. It's wrong in a jaffa cake. It belongs in a bloody drink! Time was that you couldn't make this kind of mistake. Jaffa cakes were jaffa cakes, which meant orange flavour. Now I'll have to read the small print to make sure that I don't pick up a Ponguin, Spammy Dodgers, Wigan Wheels, that ginger-flavoured horror known as the freckles cake, or the chiropodist's nightmare: twisted toecakes.

Monday 17th July: Batty Dot proved right

Decided to poke through my mother's attic to see if we can prove that my dear departed father, G. V. Jones actually did live at 63, Downland Terrace in the 1930s, and someone called G.W. Jones did not. That would allow Dot, with any luck, to claim £650,000 worth of BAe shares. Put on overalls, climbed the rickety stepladder and tried to lift the trapdoor. Very heavy, wouldn't shift.

"Do be careful, Bernard," says Dot. "There could be bats up there. They'll be in your hair in no time."

Doesn't leave me too much to worry about, I thought, as I give the lid a hefty shove. It flies open with a bang, and releases a blizzard of sooty newspapers onto my head. Restraining my Anglo-Saxon vernacular, and looking down to see that Dot was alright, I am caught unawares by a tennis racquet, still in its press, which clonks me on the back of the head.

"Told you there was bats," Dot said.

Took most of the afternoon to clear up the soot, and to actually find room to stand in the attic. Enough old newspapers up there to wrap a nation's fish and chips. Parchment fragments of forgotten England: Hoare Belisha and his beacons, Sir Gerald Nabarro and his road accidents, Profumo and his indiscretions, George Brown and his bottle. Then there was foreign policy: Malaya, Suez, Aden, Rhodesia. All forgotten now. Bundled up a few likely looking files of papers and set off home. Mother is 90 tomorrow. Would be wonderful if I could get her some good news by then.

Elevenses: Three slices of battenburg, provided by Dot. Marvellous! Eunice need never know.

Close of Play: Market teetering around 5700. I thought this correction was over, but FTSE is looking dodgy. I'm well down for the year, thanks to Spirent and other dogs. Only Domino's Pizza seems to have done well, up 10 per cent since correction began. Portfolio's topping is doing OK, it's just the base that is thin and soggy.

Tuesday 18th July: Birthday bash

All the family planned to gather at Dot's at 5pm. Arrived to find my sister Yvonne from Stockport waiting, huge iced cake balanced on a silver board, outside the door in the rain.

"I let my taxi go, and she won't let me in," Yvonne said. "Says she doesn't want any."

Any what? I rang the bell and heard Dot's muffled shout. "Go away, or I'll call the police. I don't want any witnesses, Jehovah or otherwise. I'm C of E."

"It's me, Mum, Bernard."

Finally, she let us in but still eyed Yvonne warily. "Who's that?" she whispered to me.

"It's Yvonne, Mum, my little sister, your daughter. Remember?"

"What about him? Is he here somewhere. The insurance man. I never liked him."

"Lance? They divorced in 1993." Finally, Dot and Yvonne got talking and within a few minutes they were laughing away as the rest of the family trooped in from far and wide. While Brian and Janet did their best to stop the Antichrist pinching all the icing off the cake, I was cornered by creepy cousin Melvin, the carpet salesman from Rhyl.

"Hey, Bernie. I hear Dot's *loaded*. Hundreds of thousands, Yvonne told me."

Melvin, subtle as a Jarvis profit warning, rarely hid his intentions. Dad, who died in 1988, had left a tenth of his estate, a few thousand, to his impoverished sister-in-law, Aunty Vi. Melvin had made the long trip purely to renew his late mother's percentage claim on newly discovered Jones family assets. While I tried to pour cold water on the chances of the money emerging, he wheedled about his wife's failing health, the terrible state of the carpet market, and the ruinously expensive underpinning they had to have on their home. Oh God, what a pain.

Elevenses: Eunice, watched me like a hawk throughout the afternoon. While dishing out Dot's cake, she gave me a slice so thin the bloody icing fell off onto the floor. When Yvonne tried to give me another, Eunice stayed her arm.

"I don't think so. We have to watch out for type II diabetes, don't we Bernard?"

Wednesday 19th July: Rabid reaction force

New unisex hairdressers opened in town. Thought I'd give it a try. Unlike the barber's, they wash your hair first. Quite pleasant until the girl bashed my cut. "Ere. Wot you done to your 'ed?"

"I was attacked. By a bat," I reply.

"Urrgh," she says. "You wanna get a jab. Might get somefink."

She calls her mate over, who was finishing drying some member of the blue rinse battalion. "Uurgh. That's disgusting," she opines, reassuringly.

"It's only a bloody bruise," I retorted testily. By now the OAP has limped over to add her tuppence-worth.

"Ooh, it's all septic, dear." She turns to the hairdresser. "My Henry got bitten by a dog in 1953. Rabid, it was. Well, that was the last time we went to Frinton, I can tell you."

Thursday 20th July: O'Riordan

Sat out to take advantage of the wonderful weather. However, no sooner did I drop myself into the sun lounger, sun hat and Telegraph ready, when I hear the sound of an engine next door. At first it sounds like a chainsaw or similar, but no, it's 12-year-old Liam O'Riordan riding a mini-motorbike up and down their drive. This goes on and on for 30 minutes. Fuming, I go round to have a word. Almost get run over by the child, who is using the street as one end of his loop and expects me to shift.

"Would you mind…," I begin, but the ginger daredevil ignores me utterly. So I ring the doorbell. For two minutes nothing happens, though I can hear the sound of loud music from within. Finally the door opens and there is sullen-faced Bethany

O'Riordan, with a love bite on her neck the size of the Isle of Wight.

"Can I speak to your Mum or Dad?"

"Nah. Ken's wiv his ex today, and Mum's shopping."

"Look. It's about the motorbike."

"Bovverin you is it?" She actually smiles a little crooked grin at this point.

"Yes, it is actually. It's very noisy. Can you persuade him to give it a rest?"

"Alright. I'll stop him."

Somewhat amazed at the ease of that I return to the garden, though the motorcycle noise still drones on for another five minutes. I'm just about to give up and go in when there is a god almighty crash, and the bike engine is raised to a scream. I rush back up to the front of the house, where 12-year old Liam is lying on his back, squealing like a demented piglet and holding his throat. The bike, throttle stuck open, is on its side. Bethany is in the process of untying a length of waist-high washing line she had stretched across the drive between the drainpipe and the gate.

"What on earth's going on?" I ask.

"I stopped him for you," she giggles. "Spectacular or wot?"

"With that? You could have beheaded him!"

"No such luck. Steve McQueen did it wiv a bit of wire on *The Great Escape*. That would've really hurt."

Regaining his composure, Liam leaps to his feet and tears after his sister into the back garden. Squeals, yells, shrieks and slams pierce the suburban peace for several minutes. Back on my chair, I leaf through the Telegraph, one ear cocked for the inevitable moment when minor affray becomes GBH, and intervention becomes necessary. How is it that I have become a de facto babysitter for these two mutant creatures?

Friday 21st July: Hawaii do I bother?

4.45am. Awoken from a deep slumber by the phone. "Hi Brrrrnud. It's Josh here. I'm in Hawaii."

"For God's sake man, do you realise what the time is?"

"It's a quarter of eight, right? Our usual time."

"For your information a quarter of eight is two, and our usual time is a quarter TO eight. The current time, for your information, is a quarter TO bloody five. In the morning. British Summer Time."

"Jeez, B'nard. I'm sorry. I guess I screwed up the time. But I gotta tell you, I'm on a coaching conference here that is genuinely life changing. I'm so excited…."

I slammed the phone down.

Eunice was staring hard at me. "Bernard, do you really have to shout? You woke me up."

"I didn't! He did!"

"I didn't hear the phone. All I heard was your bellowing."

"I wasn't bellowing!"

"Yes you were, and you still are. You woke me up and spoiled a lovely dream. I was on a yacht with Mel Gibson and George Clooney, and you were being dragged behind on a rope. It was all right though, because you had a lifejacket on. We were off the coast of some Roman ruins, in gently lapping turquoise water. Mel and I were throwing you peanuts, which you were trying to catch in your mouth. Anyway, we got bored with that and we'd just got to the bit where Mel and George were arguing over which one was going to give me a bikini wax."

"What an unlikely idea. That's enough work for two, easily."

"Don't be rude. Besides, you've no idea. You never look."

"Why would I? I can barely shave my own face. You don't ask a man who struggles to prune a rose bush to start clear felling the Amazonian rain forest, do you?"

"I don't mean waxing, Bernard. I mean me. You don't look at me. You avoid me. Especially at bedtime."

"Look, I really don't feel like discussing this now. It's not yet 5am, I've just been woken up by that appalling American, and you know it always puts me in a foul mood. And we've got that bloody dinner party tonight."

"What's *that* got to do with it?"

"Oh, I don't know. It's just that every time we see Irmgard and Nils you all end up ganging up on me."

"Oh, poor Bernard," Eunice mocked. "A big grown man, who can't defend his own point of view."

"Of course I can, but you always side with them. It doesn't seem to matter whether its about the wickedness of eating the odd cake or biscuit, the evils of capitalism, or the cardinal sin of shopping anywhere but Waitrose, it's always Irmgard laying in to me, you nodding in vigorous agreement and Nils just watching and grinning."

Eunice clearly wasn't having this. "Well it's better than dinner at the Edgingtons where you and Peter drone on about P/E ratios all the time. It's not as if either of you did much in the way of games at school."

Elevenses: Tried topping one of those appalling lemon and lime jaffa cakes with marmalade. Not much improvement to the taste, and while struggling with it I dropped a large lump of Frank Cooper's into the computer keyboard. For some reason, it seemed to make the Internet connection faster.

Chapter Fourteen

Bernard gets Swiss Rolled

Monday 24th July: Geneva believer

10.30am. Strange phone call. Sultry-sounding woman from Consolidated Bank of Geneva, said I'd been recommended to them. They were just expanding into the UK, and were seeking experienced investors for a high income fund that was due to be launched in September.

"Was that Peter Edgington who recommended me?" I asked.

"Well, the referrers are confidential," she said, but the tone of her voice suggested I'd hit the nail on the head. "They have been restricted to only one reference each. So it looks like you're the lucky one."

After I asked what this investment actually was, she put me through to a trader, Guy de Burgh. Background racket indicated some big trading room.

"Hi Mr Jones. Let me tell you about the fund. There are no upfront charges, the annual fee is just a half per cent. The yield will be determined by the tender price, but we're expecting it to be nine spot two to nine spot four at launch.

"9.4 per cent!" I replied. "How is the money invested?"

"Essentially we're talking of gold deposits here in Geneva. Now normally commodities don't produce income, but we've put the yellow stuff to work. We're able to lend this out to cover short-selling of gold futures and options."

"That sounds risky to me," I replied.

"No, no, not at all. Your capital is fully guaranteed. You see, we are insuring the commodity investors against the slight chance that they have to make physical delivery of the gold that they have sold short. But in reality, 99 times out of a hundred, the positions get closed out. The gold investors either make a loss or a profit, we don't care which, we just pick up that premium each and every time."

"Sounds brilliant," I said. "I haven't heard of your bank though."

"You haven't!" Guy snorted, then gave me a website address. "Look us up Mr Jones. Look at all the deals we've done. We've got Marc Thyssen de Rothschild on the board! We're approved by the U.S. Federal Reserve, and the National Bank of Switzerland guarantees the value of our gold holding."

"I can't make a decision now," I replied.

"Well, don't take too long. It's already clear the fund is going to be oversubscribed so we have to close by Friday 10.30 GMT. Also, the other restriction is that we cannot accept more than £40,000 per investor for the same reason. Is that a problem?"

"Er, no. No problem." I took the man's number and agreed to call him back once I'd thought about it.

Elevenses: An eccles cake.

Called Peter Edgington, and left a message. Seems he's still away. Picked up the phone to K.P. Sharma, and then put it down. K.P.'s probably the shrewdest investor I know apart from Peter, but I can do my own research.

Tuesday 25th July: Don't know which way to turn

Jemima off sick. Over breakfast announced she's pregnant! Went ballistic. How did this happen? Eunice interrupted: "I'm sure it was the usual way Bernard, let's not have histrionics about it." Turns out it was Toby, so perhaps it wasn't the usual way. Allegedly gay Toby who dumped my daughter to run off with a Spanish bond salesman called Carlos, then did a handbrake turn on the sexual orientation roundabout, ditched Carlos and took up again with Jem. This pantomime, it seems, has been going on for weeks. Her answer? "But I still love him, Daddy!"

Elevenses: Half a packet of plain chocolate digestives, while sitting in the car park outside Kwik Save.

Wednesday 26th July: Guys and doles

Huge glossy brochure arrived for me, all about Consolidated Bank of Geneva, with plenty of FAQs, pictures of the guarantee certificate, and documents with the Fed letter head. Took another look at the website. It had a clock counting off the minutes before the offer closed. I'd heard a lot of stories about scams, but this was clearly a professional bank. No spelling mistakes or bad grammar, and some big names aboard including former members of City banks. I phoned Guy in Geneva, and left a message. He called me back just as I was due to go to the Ring o'Bells for share club.

"Hi Mr Jones, have you made a decision?"

"Well I still have a few questions. There have been so many scams, you know."

He laughed. "Tell me about it. I fell for one myself, in 1992. These guys took me for a hundred thou and left me on welfare. You're absolutely right to ask. That's why we know you're the kind of guy we need. Shrewd and smart. Don't make a decision now, just send in the bank details form and the signed debit mandate. Leave the subscription form until tomorrow, when you decide how much you want to invest."

Didn't tell a soul at share club. Filled out all the forms, set my sub at £10,000. I reckon I could get another advance on the mortgage for this and still be quids-in on the difference between the 9.4 per cent yield and the 5.2 per cent mortgage fix were on. I'm just off to post it now.

Thursday 27th July: Not so Royal Mail

4.30pm: Just posted my letter to Consolidated Bank of Geneva. As soon as I let go of the envelope I felt nervous about having sent off all my banking details to a foreign bank. Just then, who should I see but a very tanned Peter Edgington. Obviously now back from his villa in Capri, he was walking his springer spaniel, Bartholomew. After small talk, he said. "Didn't quite understand your phone message, Bernard. I haven't recommended you to any bank. What was it called again?"

When I told him Consolidated Bank of Geneva, his face contorted. "Never heard of that one. Had you?"

"I looked up their website, they're quite big actually," I replied.

"Can't see why any reputable bank should be cold calling. I trust you told them where to go, Bernard."

"Oh, absolutely," I lied. I made some excuse to go into the papershop, and when I came back looked again at the pillar box. What a fool I've been! Oh God, I have to get that letter back. The collection is at 5pm. No-one about. Compared the width of my arm to the slot. Managed to get my hand in, but you would need limbs like Kate Moss to manage the 90 degree angle down, and the box was nowhere near full. Went back into paper shop and bought glue, an eraser and some string. Sat on the wall outside, tied the eraser to the string, coated it with glue, and after looking carefully around, lowered it inside the box. The letters seemed about a foot down. As mine was the last in, it should be on the top. Gingerly, hauled up the string, peered through the flap and there it was! Trouble was, the angle was all wrong, and the A4 envelope kept jamming against the roof. I tried to nudge it to the correct angle with my fingers.

"Well, really!" I turned around to see a large middle-aged woman. "May I get to the box? The collection is in a minute."

"Won't be a minute," I said and turned back to my task.

"Excuse me, but stealing the post is a criminal offence," she added.

As I turned round, the string jerked and the letter fell.

"Damn, now look what you've made me do. I needed my letter back because I haven't put the cheque in it."

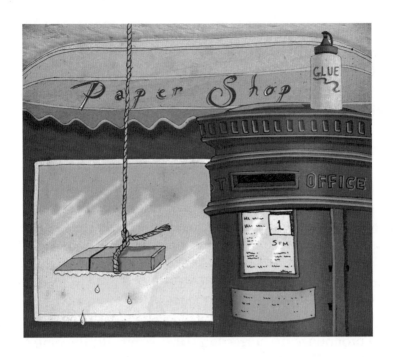

"That will save you some money then", she said as pushed a great pile of letters past me into the slot. After a final exchange of snarls and mutterings, she strode off. Two minutes later a Post Office van pulled up. A greasy-haired youth, uniform worn in the sloppiest secondary modern manner, slouched out, stared insolently at me, and opened the box.

"Excuse me," I wheedled. "I wonder if you could help? I've posted a bill without putting the cheque in. Would it be possible to have it back?"

"Na mate. Regulations. Could lose me job."

"Who'd know?"

"Dunno. You could be Adam Crozier's dad for all I know." I looked him over, and took a gamble. "Would a fiver change your mind?"

"Are you trying to bribe an employee of Royal Mail?"

"A tenner?" I whispered, pleadingly.

"Twenty and you're sorted," he said, looking around. While I opened my wallet, muttering, he looked around and opened the sack. Once identified, he handed me the letter and took the cash.

Close of play: Envelope burned, £10,000 saved. Bliss! Bought a Toblerone to celebrate. Something Swiss you can trust.

Friday 28th July: Pridgeon post

Dot's old correspondence includes a letter addressed to dad at 63, Downland Terrace and postmarked 1938. He was 19 then, and a letter from the landlord, one Mr Pridgeon, states he is the only tenant. That should end the ambiguity over the G. W or G. V. Jones. Photocopied letter and envelope and sent original to Telent share registrar's 'dissentient investor department'. Hopefully, my mother's claim to £650,000 worth of shares should be verified.

Elevenses: Remains of Toblerone.

Close of play: The FTSE100 has risen above 5,900. I think we can pronounce the correction slain, despite the ongoing Middle East fighting. Trouble is, most of my shares haven't recovered.

Saturday 29th July: St Austell here we come

Ah, blessed holiday. Going away to Cornwall for a week this morning. Brian has lent me his old laptop computer, so I can keep an eye on the City news. While Eunice buys up porcelain knick-knacks to fill our new conservatory, I can sit in the garden of our hotel, and keep my finger on the financial world's pulse. Clotted cream beckons!

10.30am. Set off two hours late. Pulled a muscle in my back lifting one of Eunice's three giant suitcases into the Volvo. Eunice opened all three searching for Ibuprofen and in so doing unleashed volcano of elasticated trousers, peasant skirts, silly fashion belts, and enough miscellaneous knitwear to stock a branch of Help the Aged. My own neat luggage, meanwhile was squashed flat. Glad I brought a tupperware box for any edibles I need to conceal.

Chapter Fifteen

Laptop Dancing

Tuesday 1ˢᵗ August: Priceless

Staying at St. Austell, or Snozzle as it is known locally. Standard British summer holiday experience. Chilly, overcast, £70 per night hotel, a view over the local Kwik Fit. Tried repeatedly to operate laptop, borrowed from Brian, to check portfolio. Bit concerned about Hornby, whose shares have been drifting down since their peak of 250p in July.

Found you need the dexterity of a bomb disposal expert to use the tiny mouse button in the keyboard. Couldn't get into the usual financial websites either. After hours spent squinting at the screen discovered that this ungrateful piece of machinery 'won't accept cookies'. Clearly Mr Dell is being prodded about cholesterol too.

Elevenses: Scone and tea with Eunice in café overlooking the old harbour. Immediately the waitress posed the 'fresh cream or butter' question, Eunice interjected: "Neither for Bernard, and not too much jam either." I feel gastronomically repressed.

Sat on a bench to read yesterday's prices in the Telegraph. The moment I lifted the paper, Eunice started on the subject of Jemima's pregnancy. "What are we going to do about it, Bernard?" There then followed 90 minutes of pointless debate until the rain returned and the paper, still unread, was pressed into service as a rain hat.

Close of play. Walking back to hotel, nipped into HSBC branch which had Teletext of closing prices. Eunice tugged me out so quickly that all I recall is Xansa, up 2p. I don't even own it.

Thursday 3rd August: Trouble in the garden of Eden

Eden Project. The best use of an old English China Clays quarry imaginable. Used to own ECC shares back in the 1980s. Couldn't understand why it failed to prosper and was eventually taken over. ECC sat right on top of its raw material, had a market for paper coatings for glossy magazines, yet somehow lost its way.

Noon: Leaving parking slot at Eden, Eunice driving today in view of my dodgy back. While lecturing me on antioxidants, she robustly reverses the Volvo into something. Breaking glass, angry yells. We emerge to see a Mr Kipling van with a broken front light, and a pile of bakery trays tipped out at the back. Enough wasted apple tarts, cup cakes and viennese whirls to fill a thousand Hornby drawers. Emerging from the carnage is 20 stone of hirsute Brummie, with a cut head. "Chroist almighty," he intones in adenoidal fury. "Why deencha look beoind ?"

"You're in the wrong place," Eunice says. "The tradesmen's entrance is there. Can't you people read simple signs?"

"You cheeky southern cow." The gorilla calmly walks past Eunice and reaches inside the Volvo. Crack! He emerges with the driving mirror which he gives to Eunice. "Here. 'Old that. I'll just remove the other bits you don't use." He then grasps a wing mirror and starts twisting.

"Bernard, do something!" Eunice cries.

"I shall write a stiff letter to your employer about this! I'm a large shareholder in RHM." This is a lie, of course.

"I'm outsourced, you pillock. I don't work for Rank 'Ovis anymore. It's the new economy and yer can't touch me."

Later, as I sit in the passenger seat with three mirrors on my lap, I reflect on the attractions of investing in insurers.

Friday 4th August: Revenge of the hippo

Awful sleepless night. Back still playing up from lifting Eunice's luggage. Fretting over Dot's inheritance, my portfolio, bill for Volvo repairs. At 2am, couple upstairs began the mother of all hippopotamus manoeuvres, working up to a choral crescendo that had the glassware on our dressing table vibrating. As I'd feared, Eunice awoke with ideas of her own. As she slid over me in a hiss of BHS nylon I knew, like all prisoners of war, that resistance would be futile. However, when it came to decibels, Eunice's sciatica and my crushed vertebrae show that agony beats ecstasy every time.

Elevenses: She must be pleased. I was allowed a mug of hot chocolate with a swirl of cream on top.

7pm: Using laptop, which suddenly burning hot on my knee. Jumped up, hopping around in pain. Yanked the mains cable out and rushed the recalcitrant device outside where it smoked like Vesuvius for 15 minutes. I think I'll go back to paper and pencil.

Sunday 6th August: Prawn free

Wonderful sunny morning, up early, free to buy the Sunday papers, wander down to the harbour and generally enjoy myself on our last day. This possible only because Eunice has Tintagel tummy and remains in bed. The culprit I'm sure is last night's 'salade de fruits de mer'. Prawns, in my humble opinion, are merely maritime cockroaches, and crayfish just pensionable relatives with antennae the size of those at GCHQ.

They cost so much because the description is in French, and you need a Paraguayan torturer's toolbox to get at them. Rick Stein has a lot to answer for.

Elevenses: Double bacon and egg doorstep with real butter, plus two fruit scones with butter jam AND cream (so there). Bought clotted cream, fudge and nougat to fill my Tupperware box, now secreted deep in luggage.

A new and exciting investment idea is hatching: Restaurants! Money for old rope, definitely.

Monday 7th August: Pig in a pipe

BP's dropped itself in boiling oil again. First blowing up its workers in Texas City, then leaking oil in the Arctic, now it's rusty pipes from Prudhoe Bay. As Betonsports discovered, once the U.S. legal system starts to get interested, things have a nasty habit of getting much worse. I have often been tempted to buy BP shares, but I keep remembering what Peter Edgington said a couple of years ago, that we should be contrarian about management cycles as well as share price cycles. With Lord Browne he reckoned, the reputation and expectation was so stellar that even mediocrity would generate disappointment and the wrong kind of headlines. I hate it when he's right, but he looks to be so, once again.

Elevenses: Two pieces of fudge with clotted cream on top, the remainder (too large for the Hornby drawer) being concealed in an airtight box in the long tunnel of the model railway. Delicious, hidden pleasures. Others philander, I just eat confectionary. So why am I persecuted?

Close of play: Why is it everyone else's shares recover but mine?

Tuesday 8ᵗʰ August: Ginger nuts

Now that I've sold the little sods, Spirent shares are soaring on stake building by its U.S. rival Agilent Technologies. Got just 33p for them on 29ᵗʰ June, and now they're 36p. Damn and blast!

"That's some particularly severe harrumphing, Bernard," Eunice noticed over breakfast. "Look, you've torn the Telegraph."

I made some excuse and went out into the garden. The Bloody O'Riordans have now installed a trampoline in their garden, and even at 9.15am the heads of giggling ginger monsters could be seen from time to time over my 15' leylandii hedge. Perhaps I'll invite Harry Staines over on Sunday. He's a member of the local clay pigeon shoot, and cracking ginger nuts would be just as easy. "Pull! Bang…crumbs!"

Elevenses: Finally fixed the lock on the Hornby drawer, inaugurated it with a packet of jam tarts. This will now be my own territory, barred to Eunice and others. Have decided to put a sign on the door of the den: You are now entering the People's Republic of Lemon Curdistan.

Close of Play: Spirent now up at 38p. Grrrr.

Wednesday 9th August: iSoft in the head

Share club meeting, first for several weeks. Nothing very impressive in our portfolio. Fortune Oil is now at 5.8p, down 11 per cent on purchase, while Billiton is hovering around a tenner, down a similar percentage. We've accumulated a bit of cash from monthly contributions, which Martin Gale wants to spend on iSoft. He's almost deafened by the chorus of 'no'.

"But it's a real bargain, now," he complained. "It's the same company at the start of the year, but now you can get it for an eighth the price." It was noticeable that one thing Martin did not say was how big a personal position in iSoft he already had.

"I don't know much about iSoft," said K.P. Sharma, "But aggressive revenue booking is a sign of desperation. Even if it's not fraudulent, it's far too high risk for us."

"What about a restaurant group?" I suggested. "We now spend more eating out than eating at home. Look at what some

City-types spend eating out. There must be something out there." I told them that one of my best performing shares was Dominos Pizza, and that other chains could replicate that successful roll-out.

Chantelle, now sporting lime green hair and a row of new studs just under her collarbones, suggested a bank or utility to get some income and stability into the portfolio.

"What about a shipyard, love," responds Harry Staines. "You'd keep 'em in business buying all them rivets. You're halfway to being a Dalek, aren't you?"

Finally, after Chantelle has threatened to exterminate Harry, I was deputed to research a suitable leisure industry share and present it in a fortnight.

Elevenses: Two packets of pork scratchings at the Ring o'Bells. Think I dislodged a filling.

Close of Play: Spirent up again at 41.5p. What torture!

Thursday 10th August: Bingo wings

Morning spent researching leisure firms. The restaurants, like Carluccios on a P/E of 30, just look too expensive. Then I stumble on Rank. It's about as fashionable as kiss-me-quick hats and Capstan Full Strength, but at 200p the P/E's just six and the dividend yield nearly 7 per cent. The more I look at it, the cheaper it appears. The Hard Rock Café, which I presume I couldn't bear to eat in, seems to make pots of money and there's all sorts of restructuring possibilities.

Close of play: Liquid bomb plot news was terrifying. I think K.P. was flying to India today. Hope he's O.K. Interesting how resilient the U.K. share market is these days. Just 30 points down in the end. We've managed Dunkirk and the IRA, I'm sure we can do without hand luggage. Besides, after my experience with inflammable laptops, the best place for those is in the recycling bin not the hold. Spirent up again, 43.25p. Gah!

Chapter Sixteen

The Bournville Ultimatum

Friday 11th August: Spiralling higher

Spirent seems to be climbing again on these bid hopes. Really cross. It's almost 36 per cent above the 33p I sold at in June. That is my losses that someone else is recouping. My money and I want it back. Don't really know what to do. If I buy now, the bid might not come, but if I don't buy, then it surely will. There is so much investment information out there, and I've got enough of it on the shelves of the den to replant the Siberian taiga. But none of it tells you what to do at a moment like this.

Elevenses: Two jam tarts with a blob of clotted cream on each. Comforting.

Saturday 12th August: Men from Mars, women from Nestlé

9am. Jemima, who didn't come home last night, arrives looking weepy. "I'm not pregnant," she announces.

"Oh, thank God. What a relief," I say, getting up to give her a hug, but she bursts into tears and thunders up the stairs. "You're so BEASTLY," she yells down.

I'm baffled. She didn't want a baby, and now she's not going to have one. Her career won't be dented, we won't have to play at being childminders. Good news, surely? Yet suddenly, there's more waterworks than Thames Water's annual spillage.

"What did I do?" I ask Eunice, after she comes back from comforting Jem.

"Bernard, look. Even though she didn't want the baby, losing it even at two months represents a loss of a dream, the end of a future life."

"A future with Toby? That's an impossible future, surely."

"Oh never mind, Bernard. You'll never understand." she says. Spend the rest of the day hiding behind the pink certainties of the FT. Even managed a surreptitious Mars bar.

Monday 14th August: The Plastic Pol Pot

9am. Knock on door. There stands the chief hobgoblin of Waste Services, one Gordon Fletcher, apparently none the worse for his battles with Daphne Hanson-Hart. Ominously, he is carrying a plastic bag at arms length, as if it were radioactive.

"Are you Mr Bernard Jones?" he says.

"Yes."

"According to official records, you were allocated the wheeled waste recycling receptacles with the following codes." From his clipboard he read out some absurdly long serial numbers.

"I have no idea. I've got better things to do than memorise bin numbers. What's the problem?"

"We've had reports of recycling infringements in regards to the said receptacles."

"I shouldn't think so. My wife's greener than Swampy."

"That's as may be." He opened up the bag and showed me some plastic objects. "I have to tell you that these were recovered from your wheeled recycling receptacle. They are in contravention of the regulations."

"You recycle plastic, don't you?"

"Ah, but this is a yoghurt pot," he said, showing me the offending object . If you had read page five of your guide…"

"So? It's made of plastic isn't it? What's more, it contained 100% organic strawberry live yoghurt. Should be just what you want."

"No, no, no. Obviously, we can't take plastics that aren't either PET1 or HPDE2."

"What do you mean by 'obviously'?".

"Look at the bottom. It says PP5. Now this one," he said, showing me a margarine pack. "This says PS3. It's well known that yoghurt pots, margarine containers and packaging for other sundry refrigerated consumable emulsions…."

"What in God's name is a consumable emulsion?"

"Quasi-solids, normally containing air. Chocolate mousse, for example. As distinct from non-consumables such as Dulux vinyl silk."

"I'm a council taxpayers, not a bloody biochemist. If don't give a flying organic fig about yoghurt pots, or emulsion, come to that. I can't read those tiny embossed letters, and I do not intend to try. Perhaps you should turn your attentions to the manufacturers, so that they only supply packaging that can be recycled."

"That's not my department. The regulations are very clear, and I'm afraid that I have to caution you that you have infringed. Now on this occasion I'm going to be lenient. We prefer to re-educate where possible, except in the most recalcitrant cases."

"So I'm to be dragged off to Hanoi, am I?"

"Beg pardon?"

"Re-education. Do you tinpot Pol Pots know what you sound like? Even a little bit of power goes to your heads. God help us all when ID cards come in."

Now I realise what Daphne Hanson-Hart is on about when she said wheelie bins are a threat to the British way of life.

Elevenses: Two Mr Kipling 'pastry-based fruit emulsion receptacles'. In a daring gesture of revolutionary zeal, tossed their foil containers in the green waste bin. How they will tremble in the halls of the mighty!

Tuesday 15th August: Councils of despair

Local councils, so I read, are now playing the foreign exchange markets with the pension funds of their employees. What an appalling thing to do, even if professional fund managers are placing the trades. Martin Gale, the share club's loosest of speculative cannons, isn't yet drawing his local authority pension but even he won't approve of this surely. It's like saying: "I'm not happy with the returns on gilts, so I'm off to the casino. But it's alright, I won't be gambling myself. I'm funding the chips for Texas 'Bob' Gunsmoke.

Elevenses: Last of the Cornish nougat. Good job the Hornby drawer is lockable now, because a bunch of grapes has been spilled across the den by a mysterious intruder. Like cluster bombs, I keep finding I've stood on one. This is just the latest unprovoked gastronomic attack on Lemon Curdistan.

Close of play: Spirent now soars to 46.5p. Grrr!

Wednesday 16th August: Astrid travel

Awful O'Riordans. Our neighbours have gone too far. Not content with having paved over the whole front garden and filled it with an estate car, a Chelsea tractor and a quad bike, I got up to discover a giant camper van at the front about the same size as a National Express coach. Not only had it damaged the plane tree on the ornamental grass strip, but it completely blocked sunlight into our lounge.

"Go and have a word with them, Bernard," said Eunice. All very well for her. Not looking forward to confronting Ken O'Riordan or his poisonous bottle-blonde wife. A quiet word with her would be an oxymoron, akin to a harmonious weekend locked in the Big Brother house with Jade Goody.

11.15am. By the time I've plucked up courage, the wagon is mysteriously gone. I walk outside into the street and there is blissful calm. No music, no swearing, no shouting. Indeed, it's a gorgeous hot day, best for weeks. Then I notice that the O'Riordans have left their front door open. I call out to see if anyone is home. No reply. Walk into the kitchen and tumble over a woman, working backwards with a mop in her hand and who, because of her iPod, hadn't heard me. She is on her feet in a second, shrieking.

"Oh my God! You almost scared me to death," she says, one hand on her heaving chest, the other helping me up. She is quite the most beautiful creature. Huge brown eyes, wavy chestnut hair, long tanned limbs protruding from skimpy shorts and T shirt, and as graceful as a gazelle. She cannot be more than 25. Getting my breath, I explain that I'm a neighbour. She is Astrid, an au pair, who arrived from Copenhagen yesterday. The O'Riordans had just left for a fortnight, presumably off blocking the minor roads of Britain in their tank. She offers me coffee while we get our breath back, and I accept. She's disarmingly friendly and chatty. I am transfixed.

"Where have you been, Bernard? Lunch was ready an hour ago," Eunice asks when I finally return. I tell her I've been walking, but Eunice's eyebrow seems to twitch.

"Oh, really. Walking to Kwik Save, I suppose to stock up on chocolate."

"I haven't been to Kwik Save!"

"And you don't have a Bounty concealed in your trouser pocket? "

"I haven't!"

"Well, it looks like you have. And you look very guilty. Don't blame me if your pancreas gives up the ghost. I've done my best."

Thursday 17th August: Sign on the dotty line

Glory be, Dot's had the letter we've all been waiting for! Dad's position on the GEC shareholder register back in the 1960s has been confirmed. They accept there was no G.W. Jones living at 63, Downland Terrace as the original register entry had it, only my father G.V. Jones. This means my mother as his heir is entitled to her 142,930 shares in BAe which were given to GEC shareholders in an asset swap in 1999. We're all rich! Portfolio problems over for good! Trouble is, who can predict what a batty 90 year old would want to do with all this lolly?

After Dot had read the letter over the phone to me, I tried to explain all this to her. Trembling fingers sliding over my calculator I told her that even at yesterday's depressed closing price of 344p, well down from February's 450p peak, her shares were worth almost £492,000.

"Oh good. That means I can get a new kettle. That Russell Hobbs is playing up again. And the tea towels are full of holes…"

"Mum, you can do anything you want. Anything! You could have that dishwasher we've been talking about."

"I told you Bernard, I won't have anything made by the Hun. Not after what they did to Auntie Vera and her macaw in the Blitz."

"Mum, Bosch is just a brand. I'm not even sure it's made in Germany. You don't have to have a Bosch, there's dozens of different types. There's some made in Italy…"

"Aren't there any English ones? I want an English one."

"I'll look into it Mum. Look, forget the dishwasher! You could go on a cruise! You could move out of Isleworth, closer to us. Anything."

"Mrs Tilly from number nine went on a cruise. And they sailed five times round the Isle of Wight. And they gave her curry. I'm not eating that African muck."

Finally, I gave up. I'll go round at the weekend. Soon I've got to bring up inheritance tax planning. I'm not looking forward to that at all. The byzantine details of Gordon Brown's tax regime are too much even for professionals, yet alone confused pensioners.

Elevenses: Celebratory bottle of champagne with Eunice. Booked a table at La Pergola for dinner on Saturday.

2pm. Wandered out into the garden. Glorious sunny afternoon, and all is well in the world. Sound of lawn mower from next door. The delightful Astrid, house-sitting for the Bloody O'Riordans next door, seems to have been cruelly lumbered with gardening. Suddenly hear a bang. Run along to the bottom of the garden where the hedge is low, and see Astrid in a pale blue bikini bending over the hover mower. Good God, what a sight she is!

"I think its broken, she said in her lovely Danish lilt. I can see it's true. She's chopped clean through the power cable. Let's see if I can help.

Close of play: I'd been gone quite a while when Eunice came out to find me, finally seeing me over the low hedge. "Bernard, why on earth are you mowing next door's lawn?"

"Their mower's broken."

"But you absolutely detest mowing. And you're not overly fond of the O'Riordans."

"Just being neighbourly, Dear."

At this moment Astrid emerged with a glass of lemon barley water for me. "Mrs Jones, your husband is so kind. I broke the mower machine, so he offered to let me use yours."

"Yes, he is so selfless, isn't he?" Eunice said looking Astrid up and down then turning a basilisk gaze on me. "Bernard. I think you had better come in now, before you get a melanoma."

Needless to say, after the venomous row than ensued, La Pergola was cancelled and I retreated to the model railway for the evening.

Friday 18ᵗʰ August: Milk float punt

Missed a wonderful piece of news yesterday. BAe Systems has landed a giant new arms deal with the Saudis. Shares jumped 20p by the close, making Dot £28,586 richer! Still, am absolutely baffled why Saudi Arabia needs all these weapons. Seems to be the one Middle Eastern country that never fights anyone as far as I can see.

Used Internet to look into dishwashers for Dot. Found Hotpoint, which I thought was a U.K. brand, and has factories here. However, turns out the firm is owned by Indesit of Italy. What on earth has happened to British industry? No volume carmaker, no lorries, no washing machines, no hi-fis. The only 'industry leader' I did find a little firm called Tanfield, dominating that absolutely crucial next generation industry: milk floats! So when the lights go out in the halls of U.K. industry, at least someone will have picked up the empty bottles from the doorstep.

Elevenses: Lemon curd tart, while I downloaded Tanfield's annual report online (you old sophisticate, Bernard). How wrong I was about milk floats! The AIM-listed firm has a bulging order book in zero emission vehicles, using battery power for jobs like airport luggage loaders, aerial lift vehicles and the like. Shares are already doing well. Worth further investigation.

Chapter Seventeen

Angel Cake

Saturday 19th August: Dot's lucid moment

Having seen the solicitor yesterday, arrived at Mum's with full documentation. Repeated whole GEC/BAe share story until I was blue in the face, and outlined why we need to set her up a broking account and start selling some shares immediately for both tax and inheritance reasons. Finally, I broached the subject of 'potentially exempt transfers'.

Dot's eyes narrowed: "You're not trying to diddle me out of your father's money are you?"

"No Mum, of course not. It's not for me, but for Yvonne, and for your grandkids Jem and Brian, and little Digby. It's just that if you pass some on to Yvonne and me now, so long as you live for another seven years, you won't pay tax on it."

"How can I pay tax when I'm dead?"

"It comes from your estate, Mum."

"But that just means you get less, doesn't it?"

"Well, yes."

"So it's you that pays the tax, not me."

"If you like, yes."

"I see, so you want me to give you my money now so I won't inconvenience you by dying, is that it? Well, it's Geoffrey's money and he would have wanted me to decide."

Dot's rare lucid moments always astonish me. It's as if the senior bookkeeper she used to be has returned, with a mind still as sharp as a pin. Drive all the way home with nothing achieved.

Elevenses: Three slices of battenburg.

Later: Bit overcast, but did a spot of gardening. Mowed the lawn. Replaced pane in the greenhouse broken by Liam O'Riordan's football. After 45 minutes Eunice stormed out, walked straight past me to look over the low hedge to next door where Astrid was sitting in a garden chair reading a book.

"Bernard," she hissed leading me away by the arm. "Don't you realise you are old enough to be her grandfather?"

"Whose grandfather?" I replied.

"Don't start, Bernard, I'm not in the mood."

Sunday 20th August: Danish tasty

Weather's gorgeous again, but garden off limits with Eunice in possession of sun lounger. Despite slices of cucumber over her eyes, she's clearly on guard. I spent the morning trying to teach myself Excel so I can put my portfolio on a spreadsheet.

Elevenses: Freed of matron's oversight I brazenly eat a jam tart in the hall, making loud lip-smacking noises.

2pm. From en-suite bathroom upstairs notice Astrid is sunbathing. Damned leylandii hedge masks all but her tanned feet…and not one, but TWO pieces of discarded pale blue bikini! Nude sunbathing, in Britain! Could it really be true? Need to get higher! Scamper up into the loft like an adolescent, heart pounding.

The only windows here are dormers almost at the apex of the roof, but I could reach one by balancing my Casey Jones stool on the tabletop layout, and standing on it. Carefully position stool to avoid its feet damaging the Unigate milk float poised to cross the level crossing, and the dozen tiny commuter figures which took two weeks to paint. Gingerly, I climb on the stool and ease window open. Eunice is straight ahead, apparently asleep. Need to lean out a bit to see sharp right over the hedge. It's awkward, but I manage.

Oh Lord! The tanned angel is fully as glorious as I'd imagined, wearing nothing but an iPod and sunglasses. She's humming to herself and twiddling her toes in time to the music. For several seconds I linger in this heavenly position. Then, for some reason, Eunice starts to get up. Panicking, I pull back. Too fast. Once the stool slips, I know I'm doomed.

"Bernard what was that awful crash!" I'm lying on the railway, my back in agony as Eunice thunders up into the loft. I open my eyes to see a mini-catastrophe. Four Great Western coaches lie on their side, one with its roof stoved in. The big tunnel is cracked as if by an earthquake, fragments of lichen everywhere. Further off, my prized Lima electric loco crashed into the water tank. The level crossing is destroyed, the tiny figures scattered like corpses.

Suddenly I feel a huge weight of shame.

Monday 21st August: All over Tanfield

Bought 10,000 shares in Tanfield at 30p. Even though current P/E is a hefty 30, the forward ratio is less than 10 for 2007, which meets the criteria I set at the start of the year. At least, being a milk float company, it should deliver.

Elevenses: Hot cocoa and a pear. Eunice is nursing me, having fallen for my excuse about changing the strip light. Still, the railway is in an awful mess. It will be months of work to get it sorted. My back hurts like blazes when I move.

3pm. Dot phoned. She says she'll sell some shares, but she wants a sports car. After 45 minutes bargaining, and my reminder that she hasn't got a licence, we settle for a mobility vehicle but: "It's got to be more expensive than Hermione Watson's."

Tuesday 22nd August: Tesco tongue pie

Awoke with back pain. Still suffering from my fall in the loft. Thinking about investing in Tesco. Not really expensive but still growing fast, especially overseas. Hardly risky plus decent 2.5 per cent yield. Trouble is, when I ever go to the supermarket (under sufferance) it's always Waitrose. Haven't seen inside a Tesco store for years. Feel I should do some research. However, Eunice smells a rat the moment I offer to do this week's supermarket run:

"Bernard, what are you up to?"

"What do you mean?"

"You would never willingly take on a chore without an ulterior motive."

"What tosh. Still, I'm willing to solemnly swear, on a packet of plain chocolate digestives, not to get anything not on the list that you give me."

Unable to work out what I'm up to, she reluctantly gives me permission. Return half an hour earlier than if I'd gone all the way to Waitrose. World War III begins the moment she sees me stagger in with armfuls of blue and white bags. She picks with distaste amongst my purchases, dismissing each in turn. "No. No. Awful. Wrong. No. Dreary. Shop-soiled." She tosses a portion of Brie back in the bag. "Well, that's rubbish. Oh Dear. And I wanted the quilted Andrex, not that awful own brand."

"It's part of the Finest range, Dear. Top quality. No chafing, and I saved £1.22."

"Bernard, not everything comes down to price. Tesco is just a bunch of jumped-up barrow boys. I don't patronise them."

Elevenses: Filled fruit meringue from packet of two secreted in glove box of the Volvo! Did I break the rules? No, because eggs, fruit and sugar were all on the list. I merely combined them in one purchase.

Close of play: Spirent, which I sold in July for 33p is now 47p. Whereas Qinetiq, which I do own, has fallen to 167p. Seen nothing of the angelic au pair next door for a day or two, but the vision remains!

Wednesday 23rd August: A bruised portfolio

Gorgeous warm morning. Hear the scraping sound of Astrid setting up the sun lounger next door. Decide there and then on a spot of gardening. Eunice, of course, comes out and spoils the party.

"Bernard why are you trimming the leylandii? I thought you wanted to block out the O'Riordans."

"Well, it's not really fair to let it get so high. It probably blocks the light to their kitchen."

"So? They didn't care when they parked their giant motor caravan at the front, did they? Besides, that's a good four feet you're cutting off there. We'll lose our privacy. They'll be able to see me sunbathing from their bedrooms and we'll…"

After a sudden pause, Eunice suddenly shakes the ladder. "Get down this minute and come into the house." I can safely say that I have never had my face slapped so hard.

12.30pm: Arrive at the Ring o'Bells for share club and everyone just stares at me. Mystified, I go into the gents and look in the mirror. Rising purple bruise on my cheek, presumably caused by Eunice's ring. What should my story be? Make up something about an altercation with a taxi driver. It is clear that Harry Staines, a veteran of many altercations from the Suez Crisis of 1956 to the 'Incident in Ikea' of 2005, doesn't believe me.

When we get down to business, it's clear no one is happy with the share club's returns. BHP Billiton is still languishing around £10, Fortune Oil is going nowhere at 6p, and Martin Gale is still bleating on about iSoft. Dividends earned since inception: nil. I report back about Rank, which I believe could be a good contrarian play at 208p. They are so impressed with its strong dividend yield and break-up potential that Martin says. "Let's buy it right now."

K.P. Sharma gets out his laptop and powers it up. "We've got £1270.14 in the kitty. How much should we spend?"

"The lot," everyone choruses. The club account is with an online broker, so Chantelle lets us into the pub manager's tiny office where there is a grimy old PC, balanced on piles of magazines. There's an Internet connection, but no broadband, and we crowd around while geriatric online snails deliver the pages at a pixel per second. Finally we get a price, already up 2p at 210p.

We can afford 596 of them. K.P. hits the buy button, and nothing happens.

"Come on, come on," Martin shouts, grabs the mouse and clicks the buy button again.

"Don't, you might buy it twice," warns K.P.
"What with?" Harry says, as Chantelle seizes the mouse. Harry starts squeezing under the desk to look at connections, and in the mayhem, the monitor slides off its perch. Martin catches it, but the cable has come out of the back and the screen goes black. After the expletives die down, I observe: "Well, we're certainly an investment force to be reckoned with, aren't we?"

Close of play: After much palaver, Rank finally bought at 212p.

Chapter Eighteen

Obstinacy on the Dot

Friday 1ˢᵗ September: Airfix unstuck

Sad news that Airfix has finally come financially unglued. I remember a major part of my childhood building fiddly plastic Spitfires and Hurricanes and restaging the battle of Britain on the bedroom floor. Ah, the reek of polystyrene cement, the tiny tins of Humbrol enamel and those sharp knives that children would no longer be trusted with. Airfix was new in the late '50s. Much has changed since. I recall buying young Digby a basic Revell kit of a sports car for his eighth birthday this year. Initially excited, the grievous grandchild tore the box lid off and exclaimed "Urgh, it's broken!"

"No it's not. You just have to build it. I've got you glue and paint and brushes. It may take a week or two as it's your first," I replied gently. The malevolent mite looked at me as if I was mad. Perhaps I am. There's nothing in his life that takes two minutes to complete, yet alone two weeks. No wonder Airfix is struggling. The only high it could offer the Playstation generation would be sniffing the glue.

Elevenses: Two all-butter shortbread from an aged packet hidden in the garage. Weather rather bad for last week. No sign of the angelic au-pair. Eunice is still in a huff, and watching me like a hawk.

Close of play: BAe Systems goes from strength to strength at 380p. Until I can eventually persuade Dot to do something sensible with her inheritance, this one share price matters more than all else put together.

Saturday 2nd September: Dotting the eyes, crossing the teas

Oh God, the Bloody O'Riordans have returned! Their huge Winnebago, fresh from giving Britain's arterial roads a coronary, is now parked in front, throwing our house into a stygian gloom. The air is thick with bellicose banter as they unload. A brief glimpse of the au pair, carrying two suitcases in. Astrid is wasted on them. Absolutely wasted.

PM: Drove around M25 to see my mother, again. Thanks to my form filling, Dot now has an Internet-based stock market account holding her BAe shares, but has so far refused to give me authorisation to deal on her behalf. We badly need to diversify her inheritance of BAe shares, but she has hidden from me the letter which gives her account name and password.

"Come on Mum, you don't have a computer so I need to operate it for you. Where is the letter?"

"I'm not telling you. You bullied me into this and I can't follow what's going on. I used to have a certificate to hold in my hand, and now I don't."

"It's a nominee account, Mum. It's safer, you can't lose your shares this way."

"So what's this Internet then?"

For the umpteenth time I try to explain, but she's clearly baffled. I have tried to tempt her with the purchase of a mobility vehicle once she lets me access the account for her, but it's no good. While she's in the loo, I do a little reconnaissance. Aunty Vi's Burmese teapot, the usual place for supposed safekeeping is awash in £20 notes each wrapped in elastic, but no letter. I do wish she trusted bank accounts. It isn't under the mattress either, nor tucked behind the cuckoo clock. Giving up, I help myself to a chocolate finger from the tin, and there it is! Can't think of a worse place to hide something from me, but in the bloody biscuit tin. Quickly, I scrawl down the account code and password before Dot finally emerges.

Sunday 3rd September: Curdistan invaded

Papers say Hornby may ride to Airfix's rescue. Nostalgia says thank God, but is it a good business idea? Perhaps if it outsources all the kit production to China as it has done with railway rolling stock. Trouble is, who is buying the products at any price?

Elevenses: Walk in to my den, seeking an eccles cake only to find Eunice allegedly tidying up. All my Excel help sheets have been stacked up, and Prescott, that insufferable suede pig has been put in my chair. "Aha! Lemon Curdistan is under attack I see," I tell her.

Eunice gives me a withering look. "Bernard, you would make a terrible criminal. The evidence of your sweet tooth is everywhere. I found two foil mince pie holders down the back of your desk, ancient crumbs under the keyboard and a Kwik Save receipt in the bin. The computer mouse is so sticky, I'm surprised you can use it."

Monday 4th September: Mum's the word

Up at 8am and try to get into Dot's Internet broking account. Password is invalid! Very strange. Am sure I copied it correctly. Can hardly ask Dot. Foolishly, I phone customer services, who respond that there is no authority for me on the account. They ask to speak to Dot, to verify her agreement and ask her some security questions. I concede that she isn't around, and they then get very officious with me. Bugger. I'm really stuck now.

Tuesday 5th September: Penny wise, pound foolish

Phoned up Dot, finally tackling her about her stockbroking account and its strange invalid password. "Have you tried to use your account, Mum?"

"You mean, the interplane thing?"

"Internet, Mum. Have you spoken to them about it?"

"Oh no. I did ask Mrs Harrison, you know, from number 66, to help. She says her health visitor, Clive, is really good on the outernet."

"Mum, this is very, very important. What exactly did you give her? I hope it wasn't the letter with the account details and password."

"No, Clive phoned up on Sunday evening and I told him those."

"Why on earth did you do that? He could sell the shares and help himself to your money, you silly woman!" I was close to panic. There's over half a million pounds worth of shares in that account.

"Don't be silly, Bernard. He sounded ever so nice."

"That much money could tempt a saint. What's his phone number?"

She didn't know. She didn't know his address, or his second name. Mrs Harrison was not answering her phone. God, I could scream. Only last week Dot made me move her Welsh dresser to retrieve a five pence piece that had fallen behind, and here she is giving a complete stranger the keys to a veritable Fort Knox of family wealth.

Elevenses: Two Curtis Teatime Fancies from the pack I bought at Tesco, and hid in the Hornby drawer. Shh! That's two crimes in one.

Close of Play: Had a brief glimpse of the angelic Astrid from the bedroom window. Poor thing looks so harried now the Bloody O'Riordans are back. Its amazing how much you can see from upstairs now that half of the leylandii hedge is trimmed to 11' or so (Eunice refused to let me complete the job). The bottle blonde Lisa O'Riordan sits in her conservatory painting her toenails a bilious metallic green, while directing Astrid to run around picking up tricycles, balls and plastic buses from the lawn. The youngest child, who I've still never heard addressed as other than You Little Tosser, is quietly pulling all the tape out of a Postman Pat videocassette.

Thursday 7th September: The mystery of Clive

Seems Mrs Harrison is away for a fortnight. Dot still refuses to let me call the brokers to change the password. Phone social services intending to ask about health visitors called 'Clive'. They said call the NHS, but couldn't tell me which primary care trust. Got nowhere in the end, which leaves me able to do nothing but sit out this enormous worry.

Elevenses: Box of fresh fudge from the bakery, on special offer as out of date. Shouldn't have eaten the lot, though. Feel distinctly queasy.

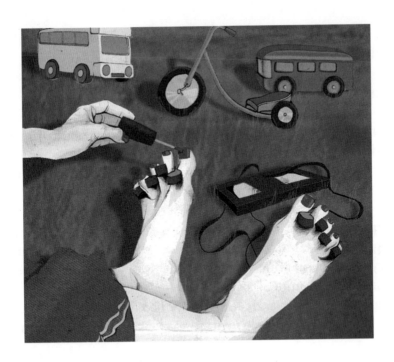

Friday 8th September: Edgington torment

Peter Edgington phones up to say a Hornby buy tip has appeared in Chronic Investor magazine. About time too, I say. The price has already moved over 240p, which is almost ten times what I paid for them. If only I'd bought more than 200. As if to infuriate me, Peter mentions that he's just bought twenty-bloody-thousand!! For my cash-strapped self the Hornby purchases are now limited to repair and maintenance activities on the model railway after my Icarus-like fall. Acquired a GWR Brake Rhymney wagon for £8.75, and a track-repair crane plus ballast hopper which I bought second hand at the local stockist for £12 the pair. Have modelled them with length of track suspended from cotton, and placed some maintenance figurines around, which makes a splendid diorama. If only my back could be so easily fixed. Eunice nagging at me to see the chiropractor, but last time it was a £45 fiasco: Twenty trouserless minutes listening to rain forest sounds on CD while an effeminate Ulsterman practised origami on me.

Thursday 14th September: Romance beckons

Breakfast surprise. Have just lifted a spoon of Sugar Puffs from my bowl when Eunice reveals she has booked a surprise trip to Paris for us both this weekend. While I'm still gathering my wits to react to this alarming piece of news, she begins her pitch with all the smoothness of a Downing Street spin doctor.

"We've got three nights in a lovely old hotel in Montparnasse, near lots of romantic restaurants and bars. It is all arranged. Flights, hotels, transfers the lot. No need to tear your hair out trying to tap in your credit card details on the Internet, because I've already used mine. Bernard, you are simply going to love it. We've even got a romantic four-poster bed!"

Eunice's hand stole forward to stroke mine in an ominous fashion.

"That's very thoughtful of you," I responded uneasily. "How delightful."

Oh Lord. A four-poster bed sends an unequivocal message: Prepare for a safari through hippopotamus country. More coition, new and terrifying positions, but most exhausting of all the continuous pretence of passion. Two years ago in Barcelona, Eunice had put on the hotel's pay TV and forced me to sit with her through an hour and 47 minutes of noisome Iberian grunting. The camera was so close the film could easily have been mistaken for an amateur documentary about chorizo manufacture.

However, on this occasion Eunice had already moved to head off any objections.

"Now I know you always love to moan about the cost of my little trips, so I've thought of that too. We're flying out on EasyJet from Luton and it's only going to cost £1.25 each. I couldn't believe it! No wonder the big airlines are losing money."

"Well, I'm sure there's airport tax too."

"Yes, and a credit card charge. But it's still cheap."

"And we do have to get there. You have to allow three hours to get to Luton at rush hour," I pointed out. "It might wipe out the savings over Gatwick."

"It's not remotely rush hour."

"Errr..what time is the flight?" I responded, with some alarm.

"Now let me see," Eunice said, brandishing a booking confirmation. "06.05am outbound, and 23.52 on the way back."

"But that will mean we have to check in at four in the morning!"

"But Darling, I've booked a taxi so we can doze in the car."

"That'll cost at least £80! I mean what is the point of booking a cheap flight…."

"Bernard, why are you just so horrible? I try to do something nice, something romantic and thoughtful, and all you can do is complain about the price. Sometime I think I shouldn't have married you at all. Perhaps when you took me down the aisle in 1967 I should have said 'I don't' and instead sent you back to that squat creature Amelia Wrigley. And for all my efforts, this is the thanks I get…"

At this point the tell-tale sign of waterworks began.

"I mean everything to you comes down to money, money, money. You just don't care about the things I do."

"That is really not true. I do appreciate your efforts."

"No you don't!" Eunice turned her back, a gesture that I think she learned from the cat. "And, I hadn't even told you the biggest treat."

"Really?"

"There's an enormous model railway exhibition on in Paris this weekend. And I've got us both a ticket for Saturday."

Oh God. Now I really do feel awful.

Friday 15th September: Queuing for the Stelios

Paris, here we go. Alarm set at 1.30am. Of course, couldn't sleep anyway, worrying whether the taxi driver was going to oversleep and we'd miss the flight. Fortunately, he was on time. Still, a round £100 fare including tip brings this little jaunt up to the price of fractional jet ownership.

Things got worse. Deprived of two bottles of water at security and then had to pay £1.20 each to replace them in duty free. What a rip-off! Eunice lost a large jar of Clarins face cream and a lipstick to the same officious security berk which will undoubtedly set her back much more. Yes, we forgot, but how ridiculous all this security is. I mean, if the next bunch of Al Qaeda wannabees in Dagenham or Dudley are discovered to have pencilled on the back of a gas bill a plan to carry explosives sewn into their underwear, we will then undoubtedly have to board aircraft knickerless. Then M&S really would be in trouble.

Never mind that it's the middle of the night, Eunice can still window shop for England. Lost track of her by Claire's Accessories and she finally pops up by Gifts4All. All this means we are last on the plane with only odd seats left. I'm at the back next to the loo, which cabin crew are overheard referring to as 'the Stelios'.

Bumpy on approach to landing. Cockney wench in adjacent aisle seat spills bottle of duty free perfume, which she rightly calls a disaster because it's 'a stale odour'. She then compounds her error by treading heavily on my foot in her rush to the Stelios.

Arrive at hotel at 9.45am, almost hallucinating through lack of sleep. However, we are told our room still occupied until midday and will not be ready until 4pm. While our four poster is otherwise occupied, we are reduced to making a corral of Eunice's suitcases in the lounge and snoozing through CNN business bulletins. Am chased through fitful dreams by the chairman of the Federal Reserve who insists he has mislaid his long bond.

Saturday 16th September: Homage to catatonia

Awoke in the four-poster refreshed after a long sleep, to find Eunice still rasping her way through the nasal version of the *Marseillaise*. Blissful night untroubled by hippopotamus manoeuvres, helped perhaps by giant late-night Courvoisiers consumed in a little bar around the corner. Splendid time at the model railway exhibition. Fantastic double O gauge displays which have given me a lot of ideas for the layout at home. Picked up a bargain level crossing and signal box set. Eunice behaved admirably considering she must have been bored witless. Still feeling very guilty about my initial criticism of the trip. I have to confess I'm enjoying myself, despite the proximity of a) lots of French people. b) becoups de merde de chien.

Elevenses: Wander into gorgeous patisserie which is like heaven on earth, with the smell of warm bread and window displays of home-made chocolates and bon-bons. While Eunice had a café noir I devoured a paddling-pool-seized café au lait, a pain au chocolat and a marvellously squishy custard tart. Not a word of reproach was issued. What is she up to?

2pm. Department store shopping. Eunice now in full flight. Meanwhile I had my own problem. All I did was ask: "Ou est la toilette?" This middle-aged female shop assistant, lifted her librarian glasses and screwed up her face as if I'd asked for the giraffe embalming department. She then turned to an assistant and repeated what I'd said syllable by syllable. Huge gallic shrugs were exchanged, then they turned to me and each offered a volley of rapid French. Defeated by this linguistic stonewalling I finally lapsed into English.

"Ah," she said. "You are English. 'Ou est la toilette!' But of course. Let me tell you." After exchanging a guffaw with her colleague, she then proceeded to give me in machine gun speed French, with copious hand movements, directions which when followed as best I could manage led me to a dimly-lit and deserted loading bay, adorned with skips. In the corner was a bucket, which had already been inaugurated. Alright, then, when in France….

Sunday 17th September – French resistance

Last night was Eunice's piece de la resistance. The restaurant she had booked proved its authenticity by its obscure location, the Proustian length of its menus and the lack of English either written or spoken. While I studied the three leather-bound volumes, she surreptitiously looked up the descriptions in her pocket Collins.

"Oh, that's calf brains. Yuck. No, what about this one?" She pointed to another line. "Confit de gésier."

"That's duck jam isn't it?"

"No. Duck is canard. Oh. It says gizzards. Gizzard jam. Oh, I don't know if I fancy that."

Forty-five minutes later we had chosen, having picked our way around the three quarters of the offerings based on offal. How odd, when you charge enough to get the best ingredients, that you mainly rely on the slaughterhouse sweepings? Nevertheless, starters were superb and it was only my under-done steak that proved the bone of contention. After it had travelled back to the kitchen and then returned, the waiter had something to say to Eunice.

"Bernard, he says the chef won't cook your steak any more. He says he refuses to ruin it.

"But look at it. This isn't medium rare, it's running with blood! This is a restaurant, not a hyena den in the Serengeti."

The wine, however, was superb and my mood recovered after rounding off the meal with a wonderfully-caramelised crème brûlée. Only then over Cointreau did Eunice come round to the real subject that was bothering her, and the real reason for the trip.

"Bernard, I am quite concerned about our marriage."

"What do you mean?"

"Well, since you retired you have hidden yourself away. We hardly ever do anything together and our love life is a sham. You spend all your waking hours hunched over that computer screen, checking share prices and just getting angrier and angrier. Why don't you just give it up? We can manage on what we have, you know."

"But we can't, certainly not while having trips like this. We should have paid off the mortgage by now, but we just added the cost of the conservatory to it. I know the MoD pension is very good, but I didn't get high enough amongst the pen pushers to make us really comfortable. I mean if you look at Peter and Geraldine Edgington..."

"That's the problem isn't it? You want to be as well off as Peter. I don't think we ever can be, and we shouldn't try. The important thing is that we have each other, and our health."

Oh Lord, here we go. Looks like a major assault on the biscuit front. But no I was wrong.

"You see, Bernard, I don't ever catch you looking at me like you used to. Not with lust or passion or even love. And I have to say I miss it."

Lost for what to say I put my hand on hers.

"You do love me, don't you Bernard?"

"Oh, Eunice, words cannot begin to describe..."

"That, Bernard is because you never let them have the practice. You used to send me poetry, do you remember? Now the nearest I get is a scrawled note saying you are off to Kwik Save or the Share Club. Why don't you write me a love letter? It doesn't have to be anything too elaborate, just a couple of pages."

Oh God. I thought I'd finished with having to write out lines after I left St Crispin's.

Monday 18th September: Shop now, calculator

Waiting for flight at Charles de Gaulle airport. Eunice is trying to calculate the cost of her shopping with some currency converting gadget she's just bought.

Tap, tap, tap, tap. "Oh, that's good. You know, Bernard, that silk scarf only cost £1.40."

"I doubt it."

"I think I'll get a couple more, one for Jem and one for Geraldine."

"I should double check that before you race off to buy a dozen more."

"You know the brandy at the bar last night? That was 3.60 euros, wasn't it? Tell me, what is 3.60 euros?" tap, tap, tap. "£4.80. Is that right."

"No, that's definitely wrong. A euro's about 65p, so multiply 3.60 by 65p for pounds," I said.

Tap, tap, tap. "What, £234? That's wrong for a start. You have to divide by 65, surely? That would make the number smaller." Tap, tap, tap, tap. "Oh. £0.05. That doesn't seem right either."

"No, Eunice, listen. Multiply 3.60 by 0.65, which is 65 pence in terms of pounds. Come on, give me that." Tap, tap, tap. "See, £2.34. The brandy cost £2.34."

"I have to tell you, Bernard, life was a lot simpler before the euro. When it was francs all you had to do was multiply by ten and you knew what the cost in pounds was."

Wednesday 20th September: Plaudits for Bernard

Share club at Ring o'Bells. Everyone pleased with Rank purchase which now over 235p, 21p more than we paid. Actually, not everybody. Bar manager Dave Dugdale is furious that the office computer now on the blink. Chantelle, who gave us permission to use it to make the buy has been given her first verbal warning, read straight out of the Punch Taverns disciplinary bible.

Investing-wise, things on the up. Tanfield is already 10% ahead of my 31p buy, and even Qinetiq is heading back up towards purchase price. Portfolio now back to within £1,000 of where it started the year.

Saturday 23rd September: Saturday night dive

Drove round to Isleworth to see Dot as planned, though due to awful M25 traffic didn't get there until 9pm. Parking was awful, and had to abandon the Volvo in a rather insalubrious street a few hundred yards away. Prowling gangs of hooded youths round about.

"You looking at me, Man?" One yelled. I wasn't, I really wasn't. Approaching Mum's house, heard a crash of glass. A minute later her door burst open and a tall, dark figure sprinted out. I was just ten feet away. Sometimes, Bernard, action is required without fear or forethought. Tossing aside my half-eaten Bounty, I hurled myself into the fray.

Chapter Nineteen

Citizen's Arrest

Sunday 24th September: Concussion discussion

The six hours I spent at hospital earlier today gave me chance to piece together what happened last night. When I threw myself at the intruder escaping from Dot's house, I knew my chances of success were small. However I did bring him down, a tangle of dreadlocks and curses, with a sickening crash on the pavement. In the mêlée I was overmatched by this large, tough and younger opponent. Forced up on my knees, panting and with one arm forced agonisingly up my back, I looked up just in time to see Mum bring a rolling pin crashing down on my ear. "Ooh, just got him a good 'un, Clive!"

"It isn't dis one, twas someone else Mrs Jones," I heard a Caribbean voice say. "Dis one's a do-gooder."

"Oh my word it's Bernard," she gasped, looking down at the blood pouring from my head. Too winded and woozy to speak, I let the story settle in gradually. Clive had driven round to help Dot reset her official password to something she could remember, using his laptop. While he was doing so, someone broke into his car to steal his sat-nav console. He heard the noise, saw the culprit out of the window, and running out got apprehended by me. Apologies were extended all round. Clive, who is actually a qualified nurse and midwife, bandaged my ear while I waited for the ambulance.

Best of all, Dot's shares are all still there in the account.

Elevenses: Cup of vile 'machine' tea will waiting for the doctor to see me. Now I know what MRSA stands for: mechanically regurgitated solution of arsenic. No wonder so many NHS patients succumb.

Monday 2nd October: Poker in the eye

Astounding news that Congress has passed law outlawing online gambling by attaching it to a bill related to port security, and without a separate vote. What a way to run a country! Phoned Harry Staines, who is both a long-time poker player and a shareholder in PartyGaming and his reaction was unprintable. Having no involved shares, my own feelings are of the purest schadenfreude. How wicked I have become, to enjoy the agony of others.

Thursday 5th October: Spirent torments

I feel like crying. I bought Spirent in March 2004 for 82p, held them for two and a half money-losing years, finally giving up and getting out at 31p in August for a £4,500 loss. Then, all-of-a sudden this cripple doesn't just thrown down its crutches and walk, it bloody flies! First bid rumours, then improved trading and now finally today, a £50m return of capital, which has put another 4p on the shares to 58p. Why couldn't they just do me the favour of going bankrupt after I'd sold them? After all, we're supposed to cut losses, aren't we? I only ever seem to sell at the very bottom.

Elevenses: A brace of chocolate Penguins.

Eunice has announced that I need new clothes. "It's really about time for you to spend a little, Bernard."

"Seeing as you spend a lot, I'm economising."

"But look at that cardigan. It's tatty and I'm fed up patching the sleeves. Those baggy corduroys have to go too. Even your shoes, which you used to polish regularly, are now dull and down at heel. Really, you used to look so distinguished when you used to go in to the MoD. Now you're more…well, extinguished."

"I'll buy some this week," I say, and turn back to Railway Modeller.

"Bernard, *we* shall buy some. If I let you do it on your own, you'll only end up at Peacocks or T.K. Maxx."

Close of play: BAe now within a whisker of 400p, having edged up and up for weeks. Dot has finally agreed to let me use that laptop that Clive left for her to sell some of the shares, so long as I get her that mobility vehicle she covets. So now I've sold 1,000 at 393p and had the cash transferred to her bank. Not really sure how many I should sell to spread the risk of her being a one-stock wonder.

Wednesday 11ᵗʰ October: Excessively possessive

Share club at Ring o'Bells. Martin Gale still whining on about iSoft, but no-one else is listening. From the look on his face, he must have lost a fortune. Besides we've got no money, even if we did rate it as a bargain. Fortune Oil (Martin's own recommendation) had gradually slid in line with oil prices, while BHP, though altogether a more solid and broadly-spread pick is depressed by oil. Rank is our only winner. Early days, but everyone agreed we must learn what we did right and emulate it with other picks.

Elevenses: Chantelle has been put on kitchen duties as part of her punishment for letting the share club abuse the office PC so I make the mistake of buying the £6.99 special, "lamb henry, chip's (sic) and pea's (sic)". So far, so vernacular, but there's a long pink hair in the mint source (sic). Frankly, I think our favourite goth should stick to investing, she's much better at it.

Friday 13th October: A taxing conversation

A day for superstitious investors to avoid. However, it's the day when I broke even over 2006. Admittedly, the FTSE100 is nine per cent ahead, but I'd rather have underperformance than negative performance.

Elevenses: Evidence of border incursion into Lemon Curdistan. An orange has appeared on the desk, plus a j-cloth and can of polish. Fortunately, the Hornby drawer remains secure.

8pm: Phoned Peter Edgington about Dot's one-stock portfolio. Though I don't reveal the exact size, he's horrified it's all in one asset, yet alone one share.

"How old is your mother?" he asks.
When I tell him 90, he says: "Well, traditionally the age is the percentage which should be in gilts. Frankly, I'd go three ways with an equal split 30:30:30 between gilts, cash and property. She'll need the income if she goes into a care home."

"That's all very well, Peter, but what about CGT? If she sells more than about ten grand's worth she's on for a hiding."

"True, but there's indexation allowance from 1982 to 1998 and taper relief after that. You'll need advice, of course, and she'll still get a mighty bill. Methuselah wouldn't live long enough to earn out each year's CGT allowance."

"I don't know, Peter. If she sells 90 per cent, the tax bill's certain to be over £150,000."

"Maybe," Peter says. "But just consider what a BAe profit-warning would do. Better to sell half now, and take her tax on the chin rather than risk the lot. She also needs to start gifting straight away, perhaps via a trust, or you'll all get clobbered on IHT."

But gifting, as I tell him, is where she resolutely refuses to cooperate.

Saturday 14th October: Full messy jacket

The day I'd dreaded. Eunice dragged me up to Oxford Street for a bigger refit than the Ark Royal. Marched me into Selfridges, had assistants scurrying this way and that for jackets and shirts. Waved her gold card around as if she was Imelda Marco, overlooking the fact that it is always me that picks up the bill. The anticipated fight soon came.

"Try that on, Bernard. That'll be lovely for the winter." 'That' was a scarred outdoor jacket, with an acne of extraneous patches, zips and pockets: Chris Bonnington meets *Big Issue*.

"I will not. It looks worn out."

"Bernard, that's the fashion."

"In which case I should be off down the Paris catwalks in my cardigan."

"Bernard, your cardigan could make its way down the catwalks unaided. I have to put it out at night. It uses a litter tray."

"But look, it says 'Expedition Leader' on the back. What nonsense. What expedition?"

"Don't be so literal, Bernard. It's just the style."

"So lying is the style? I am not walking round wearing a lie. And who is Ultimate Endeavour?"

"It's the label."

"Why can't they write it discreetly inside the collar. Not emblazon it in embossed two-inch leather letters down the sleeves."

"You're making a *scene*."

"Look, if this lot want me to wear a marketing billboard they will have to pay. There are some perfectly good plain £70 outdoor jackets there. As far as I can see, at £160 I'm paying them £90 to wear their bloody adverts. Does ITV pay Procter and Gamble to advertise soap powder? Does the FT pay Morgan Stanley to advertise its services? Of course not, so I'm not doing it either."

Close of Play: Sat on some chewing gum on the train on the way home. Grrr.

Tuesday 17th October: Gale of havoc

Martin Gale drives to see me in a state of some agitation. He reminds me, as if any of us could forget, that he's in a hole with his iSoft shares. He bought £12,000 worth, half of it from a loan secured against his house, and has a break-even level of 285p. The shares are 50p, but today's AGM statement noted numerous 'expressions of interest' in buying the firm. Now the company's up for sale he reckons it's a bargain and is bound to rise. His request: Could I lend him ten grand to double up again? As I hesitate, he tells me he's got £22,000 of debt on ten cards, and has just been forced to sell his 13-year-old daughter's pony. Bryony hasn't stopped crying for a week. As I watch him, wondering how to couch my refusal, I see beads of sweat on his ruddy forehead and the desperate forced smile. I feel sorry for him. For Martin, this one share has become an obsession, a personal battle of wills against a price chart, in which all context and logic have been burned away.

"I'm sorry, Martin. I don't even have ten grand spare. Have you tried K.P. Sharma?"

He nods mutely, taking in our enormous new hardwood conservatory. As he leaves, coffee and bourbons untouched, he puts a hand on my shoulder. "I'll be alright," he says. "Something will turn up."

Elevenses: All four biscuits. Can't say I enjoyed them.

Chapter Twenty

Differently abled

Tuesday 24th October: Senile delinquent
With a due sense of dread, took my mother shopping for a mobility vehicle. Found a swanky specialist shop, crammed with everything from stair-climbing wheelchairs to what looked like turbocharged golf carts. This is clearly a hot new industry serving those dickey of heart, dodgy of bladder, and bulging of bank balance. Dot was so excited at the chance of causing some road rage that her dental plate dropped out and the salesman and I spent five minutes rummaging under a Rascal 889 high performance scooter to find it. There being no washbasin in the shop, I kept hold of the loathsome and now dirty object while the purchasing process continued.

"How fash ish that one?" Dot slurred, towards a sleek silver model.

"That's an 8mph model, Madam," oozed the young moustachioed salesman. "Suitable for those looking for long distance durability, high performance and some off road capability."

"Actually, my mother's career in the Paris-Dakar rally ended some years ago."

"Can I tesh drive?"

Before I could say 'no', the salesman had helped Dot aboard and guided her on the controls. Immediately she reversed over his foot, making him yelp.

"Bernard, lesh get thish one."

"Don't you want to look around, Mum? There are plenty of other models."

"Thish ish the only shilver one."

The only pleasant surprise was the price: £795, reduced from £1,800. Insurance, amazingly, is merely an option. A 90-year-old with poor vision and addled brain who'd never piloted anything more gutsy than an Asda trolley, is perfectly entitled to joust with juggernauts in an 8mph vehicle without insurance. Still, comprehensive cover only costs £57.50 for the year, so I got it anyway. Bargain!

Elevenses: Two slices of victoria sponge at Dot's. Returning home on the M25, fished in my jacket pocket for remaining stick of a Kit-Kat. What I brought to my mouth was actually Dot's dental plate, dotted with lint. My involuntary shudder at this London Dungeon exhibit had me swerve briefly onto the hard shoulder, narrowly missing a broken-down Skoda. In two terrifying seconds my entire portfolio passed before my eyes. It was all red.

Wednesday 25th October: Crumbs away

Share club cancelled. Martin's ill, Harry's hung over and K.P.'s away on business.

Elevenses: Invited to join Eunice and Daphne Hanson-Hart for coffee and the last of the bourbons. Daphne still crusading against wheelie bins, ready to die like some Joan of Arc, braised over a pyre of disposable nappies, Weetabix boxes and Dysoned dust.

Close of Play: United Biscuits, a company close to my soul, is being taken over by private equity for £1.6bn. One buyer, PAI, already owns Kwik-Fit. Can't imagine what synergies there are between jaffa cakes and exhausts, but no doubt it's just Bernard being dim again.

Another thought: Just wonder what investments I can find in mobility vehicles. Perhaps Tanfield, my favourite milk float firm?

Friday 27th October: St Trinian's Technology College

Son Brian proudly announces he is to be head of maths at the notorious secondary modern near Dorringsfield. It falls to me to show him the local rag. His predecessor, a fine old scholar with 40 years unblemished service, was sacked after being filmed on a mobile phone manhandling a 14-year-old female pupil. The film passed from phone to phone among pupils and was finally posted on YouTube. His complaints that the girl had just head-butted him, and his clearly broken nose, cut no ice with a craven board of governors. Clearly, the real training camps for technological terrorism are in the playgrounds of Britain, not the deserts of Afghanistan. It is our teachers, not the SAS, who are in the front line.

Saturday 28th October: Chocolate devaluation

Picked up box of After Eight Mints as well as a good Bordeaux for Edgingtons wedding anniversary dinner tonight. But how many years? Beyond golden, but before diamond say Eunice. Bakelite perhaps?

Chockies turned out to be shocking rip-off. An After Eight used to fit its sleeve like a banker's arm in a Savile Row suit, now they're no bigger than cuff links. It's just the latest chocolate devaluation. First Wagon Wheels shrank in the 1970s (This won't affect the tuck in your pocket, as Harold Wilson might have said) Then they chipped away the chocolate on a Club Biscuit. Now it's After Eights. Don't they think we notice? Typically tight Swiss. Before Nestlé bought Rowntree, trimming a man's confectionary would have been unthinkable.

Got home 11.45pm, with Eunice a bit squiffy and shaping up for a hippopotamus manoeuvre. However, Thames Valley Police had left a message, asking us to ring them urgently.

"It's about your mother," was all they said. Oh God!

2.20am. Finally back home. What a scare! Dot was apprehended at 9pm on the hard shoulder of the M3 at Sunbury in her mobility scooter. When the police finally stopped her she apparently said: "I'm off to shee my shun. Heesh shtill got me teef." Untrue. I posted them back on Wednesday by recorded delivery. She must have lost them again and forgotten. Wilful and demented, but so *very* rich. What can we do with her?

Chapter Twenty-One

Orchard Pillage

Sunday 29ᵗʰ October: Investing in disability
Finally got my Excel spreadsheets to work correctly. Even
wrote a formula which gives me year-to-date returns!
Unfortunately, this work out at precisely zero overall, while FTSE
is up almost 10 per cent. Maybe the burgeoning market for
disability products conceals a growth stock which can help me
outperform?

In my day, the 'differently abled' were called invalids, and
were lucky to get an unreliable, blue three-wheeler known as a
Hillman Limp. These days, the disabled are the new Mafia. Blue -
badged Chelsea Tractors occupy double yellows with impunity,
mobility scooters clog supermarket aisles and public buildings are
ripped apart to provide access ramps and lifts. Such is the clout of
the disability lobby that the entire London Routemaster bus fleet,
the capital's most iconic tourist symbol, was scrapped as not
"connecting with the disabled". Tell that to my old asthmatic
schoolmate Stan Atkins who was knocked down by a number 159

outside Streatham Bus Garage in 1968 and has carried his innards in a bag ever since. However, seeing the market opportunity is the easy bit: Where is the pure play share for me to buy?

Elevenses: Finally found that piece of Kit-Kat in other jacket. Big family lunch, usual disaster. Eunice cooked fine leg of lamb with cauliflower, but defiant grandson's reaction was: "Uuurgh." Far from clouting her monstrous offspring, Janet resorted, like so many consensus-seeking New Age mothers, to begging: "Please, Digby. Just for me. A tiny forkful."

"No. Want hoops."

"Please, Darling. We can have spaghetti hoops tonight."

"No."

Eventually she cut up his meal into tiny bits for him, each morsel drowned in salad cream. Digby even negotiated eating it on the lounge floor while watching Monsters Inc on DVD, with Janet on hand to ferry salad cream and mop up spillages. He may only be eight, but I can see a great future for him negotiating sugar tariffs in the WTO. The other side wouldn't stand a chance.

Brian, emboldened by his new head of department role is growing a beard, though if he wants to protect himself against head-butts he'll need more than that. He continues to hound me about my investment in Bovis (which at 950p is now 44 per cent above my purchase price less than a year ago!) He sees all housebuilders as latter day Genghis Khans despoiling the countryside, tearing down trees and replacing them with soulless boxes. He however, has yet to come to terms with moving to Dorringsfield, where he will undoubtedly struggle to buy a house outside the new estates clustered around the school. Things have moved on since I lived there as a boy, when you could get a detached house in Old Dorringsfield village for 800 guineas with an acre of orchard and two hen houses thrown in.

Tuesday 31st October: Incendiary rules

Shopping for fireworks. The trouble began because Densley Fields is off limits for fireworks again this year for health and safety reasons, and I decided to have a family display at home.

Many years since I'd done it, but expected to enjoy looking for two bob roman candles, sixpenny catherine wheels, jumping jacks and shooting stars, but hadn't reckoned on the new nanny state rules. First mistake was choosing the local fly-by-night discount retailer which had been set up on a short lease in what had been a branch of Currys (until that chain decided that being close to the customer on the high street was providing an uncharacteristically good service which could damage its reputation).

Entering this Aladdin's cave, I realised that all the produce was in glass cases under lock and key. The anorexic young shop assistant was so busy texting that she didn't pay any attention to my increasingly robust harrumphs.

"Excuse me. I'd like to buy some fireworks," I finally said.

"'Old on."

"I have been holding on, for some considerable time. What are you sending, *War and Peace?*"

"Eh?"

"Never mind. Can you get some of these boxes out? I'd like to get a selection."

"Everyfing's a mixture."

"I can't see them in there. Can you get them out for me?"

"Which one do you want?"

"I haven't decided, and I won't until I've had a look."

"They're all sealed though."

"I want to look."

"It's elfinsafety innit."

"I don't want to ignite the bloody things, just have a look."

My insistence brought forth an elaborate eye-rolling sigh, and extended key jangling. Finally, I chose a collection which promised 26 different rockets exploding at various altitudes, though none would surely match the stratospheric price: £110!!!

Before taking my card the elfin erk turned her vacant face on me and recited the following at a gabble: "You warrant that you are at least 18 years old."

"Of course."

"It is your responsibility to ensure that they do not fall into the hands of children."

"They've just been in the hands of children!"

"Eh?"

"You're not 18, are you?"

"I am, nearly. Anyway, the manager's over forty."

So she's allowed to sell them, but not buy them. What a curious world.

Elevenses: Cappuccino and lemon cup cake in The Coffee Shoppe. Have enough explosives under my seat to launch myself into orbit. Gives a curious sense of power. I wonder if that's how Guy Fawkes felt?

7.30pm. Oh, yes, it's bloody Halloween, the imported festivity that is replacing our traditional Penny for the Guy. Some local yobbos with black capes and skeletal face masks have just thrown two eggs at the house just because we refused to answer the door to this American 'trick or treat' nonsense. They don't fool me though, I can spot a ginger-haired O'Riordan delinquent a mile off.

Wednesday 1ˢᵗ November: Losing a fortune on Fortune

Share Club meets without Martin Gale. Mike Delaney reveals that Martin is joining the IVA multitudes to deal with his debt. Hopefully, that will finally mean that he will part with those stupid iSoft shares which are now at 43p and falling daily. I get more congratulations about Rank, which at 250p is up 18 per cent on our August buy. The club still doesn't have enough cash to buy anything else, so Chantelle, today sporting a new lip ring, makes a suggestion:

"We should sell Fortune Oil. It's a dog, and tying up cash."

"That was Martin's pick," K.P. reminds us.

"He'll be gutted," Harry says. "You can't do it. Not unless he's here."

"Look," said Chantelle. "The chances are that Martin's going to have to cash in his chips at the club under an IVA, isn't he?" If we sell some shares now, we'll have the cash to pay him back his due, won't we?"

Nobody had thought of that. But when we came to sell Fortune, we saw a colossal 5.55-5.85p bid-offer spread, which effectively doubled the loss to 15 per cent. We went ahead anyway.

Elevenses: Probably a pint too many at the 'Bells. Drive back on lanes through Old Dorringsfield. The old orchard is fenced off under a giant Celandine Homes sign! Screech the Volvo to a halt to read notice detailing 86 executive homes. For God's sake this is green belt! A huge bulldozer is squatting in the orchard, beyond which half the Worcester Pearmain trees have already gone, just stumps left. Beyond them the pear tree, thank God, still stands proud amidst a sea of mud. Somewhere on its trunk in 1961 I carved "B.J. loves A.W". Took me absolutely hours. Amelia Wrigley. Lovely, teasing, curvy Amelia. My God. All those memories, all here…

Just then, a bloke in a hard hat wanders up to me. "Interested in one of these, then?"

"No, I'm bloody not."

He shrugs, then looks back at me. "Here, are you alright mate?"

"Must be a piece of grit," I lie. He hands me a grubby packet of tissues. I thank him and flee to the car, dabbing my eyes. Safely inside, I lean my face on the wheel and howl like a child. Good grief, where did that come from?

Thursday 2nd November: Assisted passage
Celandine Homes has a nerve. Can't believe the bastards got planning permission! I can't bear the thought of 86 awful mock-Georgian executive cubby holes despoiling my childhood memories. I shall ring the council, let them have a piece of my mind. Must save the pear tree. In my heart it already has the blue plaque: 'In this place on Ascension night 1961, with the scent of blossom in the air (and after 18 months of badgering), Bernard Jones finally lost his virginity to the wonderful Amelia Wrigley.' What an unexpected parting gift, on the night before her family emigrated to Oz. Ah, Amelia. Hardly a day goes by…What might have been, eh? Still, decisions made and regretted. Can't do anything about it now, except try to save our tree.

Elevenses: Tried to find some Worcester Pearmains in Waitrose. Nope. Tesco: blank looks. Found a little greengrocer in Shensall village who at least remembered what I was talking about. Said he try to track some down for me, if I left my number. Now, *there's* old fashioned service for you.

Friday 3ʳᵈ November: Brownfield planning blues
Do you know what the council said? Brownfield! It's an orchard, I said, how can it be brownfield? Turned out the culprit was those tumbledown 1920s chicken coops at the end, where as ten year olds Four-eyes Filton, Bob Snetton and I used to race our pram dragster. Poor old Filton. Lost touch with him after school, but heard he'd been killed in Aden in '64. Died for Queen and Country. A Mini-Moke reversed over his tent in Falaise Camp, apparently.

Elevenses: Three mince pies, half of a packet on special pre-Christmas offer at Kwik Save.

Eunice seems to sense that something's up: "Bernard, are you moving house?"

"No. I'm just going through some boxes."

Eunice looked at the stack of old letters laid out on the bed, that I was riffling through. "Not going through another maudlin phase, are we?"

She picked up a bundle of letters wrapped in ribbon. "Ah yes, the lovely Amelia. She was the short one, wasn't she?"

"She wasn't short! She was petite."

"Bernard, 5'1" *is* short. I remember she was always the last picked in netball. Still, I suppose that could have been because she was bit chubby."

"She was *not* chubby. She was…curvy."

"Fat, Bernard. She'd be the size of the Hindenburg now, of course."

"Don't you have some ironing to do?" I retorted, earning a slammed door. Why is it that Eunice is not content with ruining my present and future, but tries to trample my past too?

Now angry, I drive over to council offices to see Celandine Homes' planning application. No mention of the pear tree. Looks impossible that any of the trees will survive, given how closely these boxes will be crammed in. The planning officer lets me know that Celandine must have made a killing on this plot, because they bought it five years ago before Old Dorringsfield became trendy. Now, of course, its so trendy you can't move for tapas bars, hot-tub outlets and lesbian Feng Shui consultants. I ask if I can speak to the tree preservation officer.

"Sorry, she's just gone on maternity leave."

"Who's replacing her?"

"It's mandated as 'unfilled' under the council's Way Forward scheme, until we can get part funding through Natural England for a consultant to fill in."

"Natural England?"

"It's the new name for English Nature, formerly the Nature Conservancy Council."

I give up and go home.

Saturday 4th November: Going like hot cakes

Look up Celandine Homes on the Internet. Would you believe, it's just been bought by Bovis a week ago! That might give me a tiny bit of clout, as a shareholder. First though I need a little reconnaissance. I ring Celandine itself, and express an interest in the houses at Old Dorringsfield. The woman in sales tells me that prices start at £380,000. I'm just in time as there are only eight left.

"What? You haven't laid a brick yet!"

"Most were bought off-plan by investors," she says, explaining that interest was driven by planned road widening on the spur to the M25. Due in 2008, this will cut half an hour off current commuting times. The woman is baffled when I ask to visit the site.

"There's nothing to see yet." When I persist, she says she'll ask the site manager.

2pm. Finally get to explore the old orchard. While the site manager tries to show me where the access road will go, and the community building, I want to take photographs of the trees. When we get to the pear tree, I find my carving. It's smaller than I remembered and heavily weathered. I ask him whether they plan to leave any trees and he shakes his head. There are some mature sycamores at the back which may stay, but the fruit trees all have to go. Over my dead body!

Chapter Twenty-Two

Up in Smoke

Sunday 5th November : Penny for the Bernard

In the small hours, while Eunice gargled and growled for England, I lay awake fretting about my addled mother having all her money tied up in BAe. Far from being the mature and stable firm our national defence champion should be, BAe shares have yo-yoed between £3.30 and £4.50 per share this year, which makes her portfolio and, yes be honest, *my* inheritance vary by almost £200,000. That is more than twice what my own shares are worth! It's driving me to distraction. She's really not capable of looking after the money, nor understanding what's at stake but she will not let me take charge. Dot has the irritating habit of being utterly lucid when doctors are about (because she doesn't trust them), and then she's off into la-la land when I need her to understand her own post, remember something or keep her passwords secret.

Two strategic objectives: One, get her to sell some shares and buy tracker funds. Two, get her to make some potentially exempt transfers to my sister Yvonne and me, to save us all from the hell of IHT. I can't force her to give me power of attorney, and trying but failing would backfire horribly. There is but one tactic: Persuade, cajole, and flatter. If I treat her like a queen, perhaps she will relent.

Bonfire night. Son Brian, daughter-in-law Janet and their little Antichrist, Digby, are round for the evening together with Dot. Eunice prepared the traditional bangers and onions outside on the barbecue, while I dumped a bin load of leylandii cuttings at the bottom of the garden for a somewhat crackly bonfire. In-laws only emerged from centrally-heated rooms at the last possible moment, after three warnings that I was igniting the fuse on my enormous collection of combustibles. The display was certainly loud, but even during it I was getting nagged.

"Bernard, look at the fireworks, not at your watch," Eunice said.

"I want to see how long it lasts. The box says three minutes."

"But you're missing the show. Oh, look that's a pretty green," she said as the final rocket erupted.

"Damn! Two minutes and 42 seconds…"

"Bernard, don't be such a skinflint."

"That collection cost £110! If I was a skinflint, I'd have bought a packet of sparklers. That little lot must have been developed by the same company which arms the stealth bomber."

"We all enjoyed it, didn't we?" said Eunice, brightly.

"Far too loud," retorted Dot. "Why didn't you get some nice ha'penny catherine wheels like we used to have before the War?"

"You liked it didn't you Digby," Eunice said, turning to our sullen faced grandson.

"S'alright," he said, looking up from his Gameboy. "Look, Grandma I got to the 14th level!"

I caught Eunice's expression, and for once there was a meeting of minds. We expect disappointment, but does it have to come so expensive?

Monday 6th November: Follow the money

If the UK chemical industry is under such pressure, how come that Bonfire Night now involves spontaneous combustion of the wallet? I presume that fireworks, like so much else are made in China, but it hardly seems to be beyond the wit of man to make them here. Looked on lots of websites of U.K. retailers, but didn't see any well-known corporate names. Looks like I'll have to remain with the bigger munitions outfit, BAe.

A thought just struck me. If Dot won't sell her 140,000-odd BAe shares, I can certainly sell my small tranche of 1,000 bought in October last year. That at least will dent our reliance on this one firm. Having decided, sold immediately and got £4.10 for them, not a bad return on the £3.30 paid.

Wednesday 8th November: A heart judged on a pear tree

Thinking about my long-lost Amelia again. What pleasure was the longing, the anticipation, the hoping, the lust. Trouble with today is that boys get what they want *immediately*. Sometimes at 12 or 13, before they even know what it is they do want. They're getting it from some cider-addled Tracy or Kylie who doesn't remember what happened or with whom, and doesn't care. They wouldn't know it, but the interest rate on sex deferred produces a return even Provident Financial can only dream of.

Elevenses: A jaffa cake bar. Nice, but less so than the original. Brand spreading is I think what they call it. New formats for old ideas. Clearly works brilliantly for Reckitt Benkiser and its household products (another long-standing success of Perfect Peter's portfolio, damn his eyes) but not so clever with food where conservatism rules.

Close of play. Phoned Bovis investor relations, saying I had a planning issue with Celandine Homes. Was told that the takeover wouldn't be completed for months so that I should speak to Celandine itself. I daren't even mention that it was about one solitary pear tree for fear of being laughed at. Perhaps I'll try the planning department again. I'm not giving up.

Chapter Twenty-Three

Saving Mr Kipling

Friday 10th November: Airfixed up

So Hornby really is buying Humbrol and Airfix. Risky, given the decline in the modelling market. But buying assets that generated £6.5m of sales in 2005 for £2.6m cash seems thrifty enough. However, the market is definitely spooked, with Hornby shares down this morning from 250p to 225p. While this only costs me a few quid with my holding of 200 shares, Peter Edgington, who bought 20,000 in September must be nursing a loss! From memory, he said he paid 240p, so that's £3,000 adrift. Every cloud has a silver lining….

Elevenses: Caught red-handed with mince pie in hand. "Bernard, this secretive sugary vice of yours has to stop," Eunice said.

"It's only secretive because you give me grief when I eat openly."

"I'm only concerned for your health. The doctor has warned you time and again about your cholesterol."

"Yes, but there's loads of fruit in this, I'm working towards my five a day."

"Nonsense. That's machine-processed syrup slurry, loaded with sugars and fat."

"I think Mr Kipling would be turning in his grave to hear you speak ill of his products."

"Mr Kipling doesn't exist, you silly dodo. He's an advertising voice to cover up a sinister national network of factories dedicated to silting up the arteries of the sugar-addicted masses."

There you have it: How thoroughly my wife has fallen under the spell of that spaniel-faced vegan activist Irmgard.

Close of play. Hornby recovered considerably, to 235p. Notice Tanfield performing superbly too. From 30p to 42p in just three months. Who said milk floats can't accelerate?

Friday 17th November: Bernard's first ten-bagger

Hornby results received well, shares completed remarkable recovery to 270p, which now makes it officially a ten-bagger from my 26p buy price in 2001. However, my £488 actual profit is infuriatingly small. Perfect Peter's gains since he bought in September are now an irritating £6,000. Even in my own area of expertise, I'm outmatched.

Elevenses: A plate of crisps has mysteriously appeared on the desk in Lemon Curdistan. Highly suspicious! No idea what type, no bag to check. Odd aroma, perhaps sautéed vole? Knowing Eunice they are likely to be a cunning twist on a known flavour, like beef and mustard gas, or pickled bunion. Perhaps she's been taking tips from the KGB. First Litvinenko, now me! After ignoring them for a half hour, I am unable to resist the lure of vole, and eat a morsel. Quite pleasant, consume remainder.

Close of play. I can hear a recently-arrived Eunice in the kitchen. Emerging silently across the Curdistan border, I notice the

Waitrose bags in the hall. Flitting from shadow to shadow, I flatten myself behind the kitchen door.

"Enjoy the crisps, Bernard?" Eunice says.

I hold my breath. How on earth does she know?

"There's no point hiding, Dear. I can smell the rubber from your new slippers."

The horrifying story emerges. It appears I have ingested a lethal dose of a substance known only to a few in the security services. It is a kind of Lincolnshire ginseng, known by the code word 'parsnip'. This rare root can masquerade as real crisps by being thin sliced and then deep fried. Finally, she lets me know who is the culprit.

"Irmgard made them specially. Hardly any salt, lightly fried in sesame oil and with eight per cent fibre, they'll be perfect for elevenses. So come on, hand over the key to the Hornby drawer. Your cake days are over."

Tuesday 14th November: Planning oversight

Celandine Homes insists that it isn't possible to save any of the fruit trees because of the stone sets they are planning for the driveways. Right, we'll see about that. Go to the planning office in person and read every turgid word of the old orchard planning application. No mention of the fruit trees at all. So I ask the planning officer whether a planning application would have to note any trees that they plan to fell. The answer is yes, so long as said greenery is more than 1.5 metres high and 10cm in diameter. I point out to him that the Old Orchard was full of trees of at least this size, and some remain. Eyebrows are raised. Notes scribbled. Phone calls made. I see the wheels of bureaucracy finally begin to turn! I ask if I can make an application for a preservation order on one tree in particular. I am handed forms to fill in. Perhaps, just perhaps, my council tax payments aren't wasted after all.

Elevenses: Sitting in the Volvo opposite the old orchard, with the heater on, and a copy of Chronic Investor to disguise my surveillance. I see the pear tree is still there, thank God. I open the glove compartment, and help myself to a fresh cream éclair. This is going to have to be the new Hornby drawer in exile, now that Lemon Curdistan is under the enemy boot.

Chapter Twenty-Four

Flight of Angels

Monday 4th December: Quornered

Another food merger. After losing out in its attempt to get hold of United Biscuits in October, Premier Foods has now tried to swallow RHM, maker of Mr Kipling cakes (and by Royal appointment, supplier to Bernard Jones). RHM has twice the sales of Premier, but because of a lower market value could be digestible by the smaller firm. But what could it be about Angel Delight, Quorn, Branston Pickle and Smash that makes Premier worth so much more at £1.4bn than the £900m pre-bid value accorded the maker of Bisto, Mr Kipling and Mothers Pride (the only bread that the Antichrist will consider for his salad cream sandwiches)? RHM's gross margin is higher, its net margin is the same and it boasts a better dividend. It even has less debt. So why is it worth less? Baffled.

Elevenses: A Mr Kipling mince pie, something of a bitter-sweet moment as the brand changes hands. I do hope they don't mess with the recipe and fill it with Quorn. After all, we know what Nestlé did to After Eights.

Wednesday 13th December: Party time

Investment club Christmas knees-up. The Ring o'Bells is packed. Martin Gale in better spirits after his IVA, which hasn't so far even required him to surrender his stake in the club. Though Martin pleads poverty when it's his round, he still expects to drink like a fish. Get to discussing food companies with Harry Staines, who says he just made a festive food investment in InterLink Foods.

"Weren't they the ones who had a profit warning?" I asked.

"Ah, but that's what makes them cheap. They make 120 million mince pies a year, so the dosh should be pouring in now."

K.P. Sharma has had a double whisky and is now wearing a Santa hat and waving mistletoe about.

Thursday 21st December: Raiders of the lost cause

Unbelievable evening. Eunice at an old girls' reunion at Wigmore Hall, marking forty years since leaving St Celia's Girls Academy. A more terrifying gaggle of Amaretto-marinated nymphomaniacs you would be hard pressed to find. She said she'd stay with Angharad in Pimlico if she missed the last train. So as the rain slashed down outside, I settled down with a glass of Islay to watch the life history of Brunel that I'd recorded from BBC2.

11.30pm. Doorbell went repeatedly. Surely Daphne Hanson-Hart hadn't reversed into our gatepost *again* . However as I walked into the hall, a glance through the glass revealed this wasn't Daphne, nor Eunice. I opened the front door and a sobbing Astrid, wearing only a bathrobe threw herself into my arms.

"Please, Mr Jones. Help me. Mr O'Riordan attacked me."

I saw she had a cut foot, and ushered her in.

"I lock myself in bathroom, and climbs out through window. But I broke vase…sorry, my English is terrible now."

"Well, you'll be safe here. Come, on let's get that foot sorted out," I said gently. I got a tea towel from the kitchen, wrapped up her bare foot, and then helped her upstairs. I sat her on the side of the bath while I washed, bathed and bandaged that beautiful foot. Once I'd got her a brandy she told me the full story. Ken O'Riordan had dispatched his wife to a spa as a pre-Christmas gambit, and once Astrid had put the children to bed he suggested they watch a film together. Poor innocent Astrid thought the title was *Raiders of the Lost Ark*, but realised her mistake the moment the first naked posterior wobbled into view. Seeing her expression, Ken complained that as a Dane she shouldn't be ashamed of her nation's greatest export. He pinned her on the sofa, and when he tried to pull her bathrobe open, she used a knee to good effect and fled upstairs. Now, as I stared into those almond-shaped brown eyes, brimming with tears, I saw pure trust. I couldn't let her down.

"Astrid, you don't have to go back. Not at all. I'll call the police…"

"Please, no. I don't want big trouble. I just have to get my things. My iPod is there…"

"Look stay here tonight. I'll go and get your things first thing tomorrow morning when he's sobered up, then we can go to the police afterwards."

I found her some of Jemima's spare pyjamas (choice of rabbits, elephants or heart pattern). A thunderous pounding on the front door interrupted us.

"That's him! Oh God!" Astrid shrieked.

"Leave him to me," I said, feeling far less confident than I hoped I sounded. Through the green glass door panel I could see O'Riordan, all 6'3" and apparently a body double for the Incredible Hulk.

"I know she's there, Jones," he growled. "This door opens in five seconds, or I'll rip it from the frame. Your choice."

There was no doubt he meant it. I picked up the only weapon to hand, a Dambusters memorial wall clock that Eunice's late mother had given us in 1983 to mark forty years since the raid. It was certainly a nasty piece of tat, but would it be nasty enough?

"Right," O'Riordan boomed. "Five, four, three, two...."

There was no doubt Ken O'Riordan would have demolished the house to get at Astrid, but I wasn't going to open the door. I gripped my weapon like a discus. Then, just as Ken's countdown for me to open the door reached one, I heard a child yell.

"Dad, who are you shouting at?"

Ken's comprehensive list of expletives was followed by: "Go to bed, Bethany."

"But we can't sleep. Mum's on the phone. And Little Tosser's wet the bed again."

The groan beyond the front door was one of total defeat. As Ken slouched away, defeated by the weight of family demands, Astrid again asked me not to call the police. Instead, we talked for two delightful hours, and drained the best part of half a bottle of brandy. At 3am I shepherded a giggly Astrid up to Brian's old room. I drew the curtains and said a gentle goodnight.

"Mr Jones."

"Please, call me Bernard."

"You have been so kind. You are a real gentleman. Thank you." She leaned forward, and though I went for a cheek she moved her face and kissed me gently on the lips. I was surprised that it was I who pulled back first.

"My brave knight in armour," she murmured. For five very long seconds we stared into each other's eyes. I knew then what *could* happen but must not.

"Sleep well," I said and left.

Friday 22nd December: Rendezvous with destiny

6.30am. Awoke, and unable to get back to sleep. Went into the den. For the sake of distraction, trawled some financial websites. Read some rather dull stock market reports covering Tokyo, Taipei and Seoul. Companies I'd never heard of, results I didn't care about, and the odd profit-warning, hitting investors whose faces I would never see. The one face I could not banish, as I turned away from the screen was one with the finest cheekbones, a perfect smile and dazzling brown eyes, wide with trust. Asleep just a few short steps away.

8am. Tried to focus on the paper. Vodafone is bidding $13bn for some Indian cell phone company. Why are these mobile phone groups so desperate to keep expanding? After Mannesman and the billions of write-offs, you would think that they would have learned the lesson. For shareholders at least, bigger is not necessarily better, especially when a bidding war is likely to result in overpayment. As someone with a cordial dislike for mobile phones, investing in the damn things has been one of few money-losing vices that I have not experienced.

Oh God. I hear Eunice reversing into the drive. My heart has started to pound wildly.

"Have a good time, dear?"

Seeing her face, I knew she had not.

"That awful Angharad, remind me not to stay with her again. Just because she's remarried some bloody Yankee banker at Morgan Stanley she thinks she's better than anyone else." She stopped, hearing the sound of the power shower. "Is Jem here?"

"No dear, there was a bit of a to-do next door last night and Astrid, you know, the au pair, came here seeking asylum."

"Bernard, I know *full* well who Astrid is." Eunice's eyes were as cold as stone. "So she stayed here?"

"Only in Brian's room, Dear," I squeaked.

"...On the one night in the last 18 months when I did not." She sniffed deeply, as if to detect in the air of the house some scent of mischief or pleasure, some dab of dalliance. Unable to meet her gaze, I made Eunice some coffee and told her Astrid's tale.

"So you see, I could hardly turf her out, could I?"

At that moment Astrid came down stairs, tousled hair cascading over the bathrobe. Eunice changed completely, clucking and fussing and sympathising: "Poor thing....how horrible for you...We never liked him you know...let's get this bloodstained robe washed." After taking her upstairs to find something wearable among Jem's clothes, Eunice returned to me, sympathy face switched off.

"I'll just say this, Bernard. You have probably been very gallant. But if you have been in any way unfaithful to me with that young lady, I shall kill you. Do you understand?"

Christmas Eve: Joining up the Dots

Went round to collect Dot for Christmas. While crawling back round the M25, I again tried to persuade her to diversify her BAe shares, this time through a selective, lurid and beautifully spun tale about Al Yamamah kickbacks. Alastair Campbell would have been proud of me.

"So you see, I'm not convinced that BAe is a very ethical place to have your money, Mum. Guns, bombs, bribes, all that stuff."

"But they make Spitfires don't they?"

"No, Mum. No-one makes Spitfires any more."

"So why am I saving my old saucepans?"

"I didn't know you were."

"I've got a cupboard full, but the War Office has never come for them. Well, if that's their attitude, let's get rid of them then, the shares and the saucepans. Sell the lot."

Lord be praised! She's finally seen sense.

8pm. Escape the family hubbub and Channel Five repeats downstairs, and climb up into the tranquillity of the loft. The model railway is well under repair, a diorama of new track and gravel being laid, with small painted figures helping with the lifting and bedding. Standing on the stool I open the skylight and cool night air floods the room. Somewhere in the distance an owl hoots.

★ ★ ★

Astrid got her possessions back easily enough. Eunice went straight round to see Lisa O'Riordan the moment she returned from the health spa. Ken had clearly wasted his money. The calm and relaxation of Lisa's detox and aromatherapy sessions evaporated like snow on the slopes of a erupting volcano. Long after Eunice returned with Astrid's suitcase and rucksack, I could still hear yelling and the sporadic mortar fire of mugs and cups ricocheting around the O'Riordan kitchen while a shame-faced Ken remained in the conservatory, resolutely glued to Sky Sports and its coverage of women's bowls.

Ignoring Eunice's scowl, I took Astrid to the station rather than have her limited finances strained by a taxi fare. Couldn't let her leave on her own after such a terrifying experience. I carried her bags through to a desolate and windswept platform, the first stage of a long journey that would take her via friends in London back to Copenhagen for the New Year.

"I'm sorry that your short experience of Britain has been so awful," I said.

"Don't apologise. Not everyone here is like Mr O'Riordan," she said, as the wind blew her rich chestnut hair across her face. "There have been some very good experiences too." She smiled and flicked her scarf gently across my chest, a curiously intimate gesture.

The train arrived and I helped her on with the bags.

"Goodbye then, Astrid."

She turned and gave me a big hug. "Thank you for what you did last night when I was upset and needed help. You were strong for me. And thank you, too, for what didn't happen. Then you were strong for both of us. That makes Bernard Jones a rare and special man."

The doors closed and with agonising slowness the train pulled away. I watched Astrid waving through the window. The last thing I saw was her blowing me a kiss. As I turned back to the platform, a gust of wind sent crisp packets and chocolate wrappers spinning in eddies, Coke cans rattling in the gutters. I turned up my collar through habit, but felt no chill. A radiating warmth coursed through me, spilling into an uncontrollable grin. Even at 63, it's not too late to find out what you're made of. Even nicer to be agreeably surprised.

I think I've earned a chocolate digestive.

If you didn't enjoy this book, it's highly unlikely that you will appreciate the second volume of The Investment Diary of Bernard Jones either. Still, in case you are unsure, here on the following pages is a sample chapter from *Bernard Jones and Temple of Mammon*, which is scheduled for publication by Ludensian Books in November 2007.

ISBN 978-0-9554939-1-1

www.nicklouth.com   www.bernardjones.co.uk
www.ludensianbooks.com

Bernard Jones and the Temple of Mammon

Volume II of The Investment Diaries of Bernard Jones

New Year's Eve: Thompson twinge

Having lost six per cent on 2006, Hell's Bells may be one of the more ramshackle share clubs in terms of performance, but I like to think we get our dividends in fun. Our New Year's party at the Ring o'Bells went with a swing, partly because most of us have been let off the family leash for the evening. However, the one 'other half' who did attend was Mrs Sharma, looking resplendent in a glittering green sari and half moon specs. As the pub couldn't get kitchen staff, she supplied most of the food, including the notorious thermonuclear samosas. However the tandoori lamb was divine, and the fish madras with lime quite exquisite. Still, such fare needs plenty of lubrication and after three pints of hand-pulled Spitfire I went on a rather wobbly sortie to the toilet.

Lurching through the door, I see it's been refurbished in lime green (do I detect Chantelle's tastes here?). The moment I reach my destination, there is a hiss and something that smells like Tom Jones's aftershave is squirted about me. Looking up I see the skull-like 'fragrance disperser' and the dread emblem of Rentokil Initial. Similarly emblazoned is the (empty) soap dispenser and the (non-working) hand-drier.

Rentokil was one of my first and worst share forays, as I fell under the spell of one Clive (now Sir Clive) Thompson, a.k.a Mr Twenty Percent. I bought in the middle of 1998 at about 400p when the firm could do no wrong, spilling out profits faster than paper towels from a badly-fitted dispenser. Soon however, growth came as reluctantly as sheets of toilet paper from those big metal drums which are designed to stop the theft of the roll, and on which I once cut my knuckles at Gatwick Airport. I eventually sold at 225p, having missed the brief chance to sell at 475p in the 2000 bubble. The collapse of Sir Clive's low income savers firm Farepak last year brought back distasteful memories.

Now the final Thompson challenge. A new washbasin has replaced the cracked old thing which always leaked. However, its shiny minimalist taps (labelled F and C: Did the pub try to save money by ordering surplus Congolese or Paraguayan versions?) have no obvious mode of operation. Nothing to twist. No foot pedal. I press tap C. Absolutely rigid. I try waving my hands in front in case they are cunningly infrared operated, which in the mirror makes me a Tommy Copper impersonator (just like that). But still nothing. At this moment Harry Staines lurches in, cannons off two walls and into the cubicle, whose door he leaves open as he does his Victoria Falls impersonation.

"Do you know how these work, Harry?"

"I never trust a tap," he says enigmatically as he strides out to join the great unwashed.

Finally, I press the top of the other tap. Instantly a ferocious spray of freezing water (so that's what the F stands for) hits me at trouser height. After some anglo-saxon vocal exercises, I find there is absolutely nothing, neither towel, curtain nor sheet of toilet paper in this Rentokil khazi to dry out these embarrassing dark patches.

Furtively, I emerge in search of beer towels and run straight into Mrs Sharma, who takes one trouser-ward glance and flees. Oh God! I think Sir Clive has cursed me.

Wednesday 3rd January: Vintage misery

Edgington dinner party on Saturday. Peter's scribbled message on the invitation said "celebrating a vintage year in 2006." He's bound to gloat about his share-picking performance. I find this too depressing for words.

Elevenses: Eunice and I had a huge row about cholesterol and diet over Christmas culminating in her flouncing off to spare room. Three days of bliss, safe from snoring and dreaded hippopotamus manoeuvres. However, the final compromise forced on me is to give up the Hornby drawer key, though I can still (for now) eat what I like.

Close of Play: Down £270, second loss in a row. I thought January was supposed to be a good month.

Thursday 4th January: Share checkers anonymous

After a first day frenzy, the market seems to have gone soggy. However, I'm going to try to make a New Year resolution of only checking share prices three times a day. Once at the open, once at elevenses, and once at close of play. That's really perfectly adequate. Yet I have to admit the lure of that little screen portfolio tool is very strong. While I'm trying to research what I should buy this year by doing some fundamental research, I have developed this crackhead's habit of doing a sneaky click to see if Domino's Pizza or BAe have added 1p or lost 1p in the last ten minutes. Who cares, Bernard? You are in for years not weeks, yet here we go again. Click. BAe up 2p.

Elevenses: Now, here's a curious thing. Came to eat last eccles cake from drawer and found a small self-adhesive red dot on it. What on earth does this mean?

Sunday 7th January: Perfect Peter entertains

Edgington dinner party last night, saw Peter at his most nauseating. While Geraldine showed Eunice her collection of Edwardian jewellery, Peter walked me through his successes for 2006, most of which seem to have soared AND pay big dividends: Scottish & Southern Electricity, Viridian, Irish building products firm Kingspan, HBOS, Northern Rock, and Persimmon. Had he lost money on anything at all, I wondered?

"Almost," he said. "I made very little when I sold BG Group. However, it was clear that wholesale gas prices were going down from about August, so I would have lost out had I waited."

How awful for him. To NEARLY lose money.

Elevenses: A plain chocolate bounty. As I opened it, I saw it had been labelled with an orange stick-on dot. What can this mean?

Monday 8th January: The Quatermass experiment

Peter's successes seemed all to come in value stocks, the flavour of the year 2006. Can hardly continue surely when dull old electricity firms rise by 50 per cent in a year. Also read a piece of research from the U.S. which said that the shares covered by the fewest analysts did best. Now we know just how overpaid those chinless City wonders are. When Goldman Sachs initiates coverage we should probably sell.

Elevenses: A curious green finned fruit-like object has materialised in the Hornby drawer. There's no obvious fuse or explosive charge, but it does sport a green adhesive dot. I leave Prescott, Jemima's suede pig, to guard it while I seek enlightenment from on high.

"It's a star fruit, Bernard. You must have seen them," Eunice said.

"It's more like something Dr Quatermass dreamt up on an off-day," I retorted. "What am I supposed to do with it?"

"Eat it in slices. It's full of vitamin C. That's why I gave it a green light."

"Green light. Ah! Is that what those silly dots are all about?"

"They're not silly, that's the government traffic light scheme to label food according to how healthy it is."

"I know, but if the supermarkets don't want it, why should you impose it within the household?"

"Supermarkets don't want it for obvious reasons. They want people to buy fatty foods because they are more profitable."

"Supermarkets don't reveal their profit margin by product. It's a closely guarded secret. Don't tell me you've been doing some share research of your own?"

"Don't be facetious, Bernard. It's perfectly obvious. Fresh foods are an open book. An apple, a parsnip or a carrot has a value the shopper can relate to. They couldn't charge us £1 each because we'd know from common sense it's too much. Yet who knows what arcane processes go in to making a packet of Hula Hoops, a sausage or a one of your precious eccles cakes? The truth is that we think we know the right price, yet the cost of ingredients is far less than we suspect because of cheap sweeteners and industrial hydrogenated fats."

"You're ignoring the fact that supermarkets don't make their own products," I said.

"Of course. They buy them in cheaply. Anyway, I really don't want all that rubbish clogging up your arteries. That is why I have started labelling your elevenses."

Eunice oversees me as I eat the thing. It has a curious waxy texture and is mildly sweet, but I can't escape the worry that I'll swell up like the Elephant Man and be sent to intensive care.